BEYOND
FORT MIMS

LAURAN PAINE

SAGEBRUSH
Large Print Westerns

First published in the United States by Center Point

First Isis Edition
published 2017
by arrangement with
Golden West Literary Agency

A catalogue record for this book is available
from the British Library.

ISBN 978–1–78541–388–9 (pb)

Published by
F. A. Thorpe (Publishing)
Anstey, Leicestershire

Set by Words & Graphics Ltd.
Anstey, Leicestershire
Printed and bound in Great Britain by
T. J. International Ltd., Padstow, Cornwall

This book is printed on acid-free paper

BEYOND FORT MIMS

In the Alabama compound of Fort Mims, over five hundred people — soldiers, women and children — go about their business, unaware that the place is surrounded by a force of Creek Indians. As the call to muster sounds, over one thousand warriors descend upon the walls, and proceed to overrun the fort and massacre the inhabitants. In response, a militia is raised to fight. One of those who enlists is David Crockett, a young husband and father — and a renowned hunter. Serving with the Winchester volunteers, Crockett builds up his reputation as a first-rate scout and shooter. However, his responsibilities are not confined to those of the military life. Between his spells of service, he must also ensure that his family is kept safe and fed, and his land defended from not only hostile Indians, but also ruthless frontier renegades.

SPECIAL MESSAGE TO READERS

THE ULVERSCROFT FOUNDATION
(registered UK charity number 264873)

was established in 1972 to provide funds for
research, diagnosis and treatment of eye diseases.
Examples of major projects funded by
the Ulverscroft Foundation are:-

- The Children's Eye Unit at Moorfields Eye Hospital, London
- The Ulverscroft Children's Eye Unit at Great Ormond Street Hospital for Sick Children
- Funding research into eye diseases and treatment at the Department of Ophthalmology, University of Leicester
- The Ulverscroft Vision Research Group, Institute of Child Health
- Twin operating theatres at the Western Ophthalmic Hospital, London
- The Chair of Ophthalmology at the Royal Australian College of Ophthalmologists

You can help further the work of the Foundation
by making a donation or leaving a legacy.
Every contribution is gratefully received. If you
would like to help support the Foundation or
require further information, please contact:

THE ULVERSCROFT FOUNDATION
The Green, Bradgate Road, Anstey
Leicester LE7 7FU, England
Tel: (0116) 236 4325

website: www.foundation.ulverscroft.com

CHAPTER
ONE

Fort Mims And Beyond

The fort was a large, palisaded compound, its inhabitants, including eighty militiamen under Major Daniel Beasley, included five hundred and thirteen people among whom were one hundred and eighty women and children. Normally the gates were left open during the day. The surrounding cleared land was deep and rich and because of high humidity and frequent rains crops were bountiful, cattle were grazed, and harvested produce was stored.

The late summer of 1813 was one of the hottest on record for Alabama. Rains were infrequent but humidity remained high. Fort Mims was roughly thirty miles from Mobile Bay where the Mobile River flowed into Mobile Bay, which was about thirty miles north of the Gulf of Mexico. The entire area over many miles, with or without rain, had high humidity.

On a serene Sunday church services were in progress for those who attended. For those who didn't there were wrestling matches, drinking, loafing, and whatever form of relaxation people sought in fiercely hot and humid weather.

A slave named Hosiah was foraging outside the fort when he saw Indians. Hastening back to the fort, he told his owner, John Randon, what he had seen. Randon went immediately to Major Beasley, who had just finished a wrestling match with a captain of militia named Dixon Bailey.

The major, who had been drinking, listened to what Randon had to say, and because Randon seemed sincerely worried Beasley agreed to send out scouts. He also promised that if Hosiah was lying, he would be whipped.

The scouts left the fort, sought shade from the heat, and eventually returned to report no sign of Indians.

The anxiety caused by Hosiah's tale diminished as time passed and the major's assurance that there were no Indians in the vicinity was supported by the general knowledge that there had been no Indian trouble, except isolated, mostly distant incidents in a long time.

Sunday passed comfortably for the fort's inhabitants. It would be the last for many of them. Hosiah had not lied. An Indian called Red Eagle, whose given name was William Weatherford, the son of an Indian woman and a Scotsman named Lachlan McGillivray, and who the Creeks called Hoponika Fitshia, Truth Maker, had Fort Mims completely surrounded.

Monday morning Red Eagle had made his final disposition for the attack. The signal would be when the soldiers inside the fort were summoned to their midday meal by a drum roll.

At the time of the drummer's call to mess, Major Beasley was playing cards with some officers. At the sound of the drum Red Eagle and his one thousand yelling Indians broke from cover and raced toward the fort.

There was a rush to close the gates — too late. Hundreds of Indians firing muskets, arrows, and holding aloft tomahawks and clubs streamed inside.

As Major Beasley ran toward the blockhouse, he was overtaken by an Indian with a stone tomahawk who killed him with a blow that split his skull.

Captain Dixon Bailey tried to rally the soldiers as Indians were pouring through the gates. Some inhabitants, mostly women and children, made it into the blockhouse. The children were put in the loft; on the ground floor women reloaded guns.

Outside was pure chaos. Indians clubbed, shot, and knifed indiscriminately children, women, old people, men, even small animals. Captives were put to death by torture. Their screams could be heard above the bedlam inside the blockhouse.

Repulsed by gunfire from the blockhouse, the Indians turned to clubbing the dying. At this juncture the Indians found the liquor stores. Afterward, they went on a particularly gruesome rampage of killing, scalping, and even killing again those already dead. Several heads were cut off and the Indians used the heads for a kind of soccer game.

When the fighting dwindled until only those in the blockhouse still offered resistance and fired their weapons selectively, probably because their powder and shot was diminishing, Red Eagle and most of his warriors left. The remaining Creeks, with no reason for haste, spent what remained of the day plundering, torturing and killing captives, drinking, and celebrating their victory.

For them the final tragedy was inevitable and there was no reason to hasten it. Inside the blockhouse were people unable to escape, unlikely to be saved, and for those reasons plus one other — fire — there was no need for the Indians to take risks.

The number of escapees was about half a dozen. One black woman named Hester, although wounded, got past the fighters, reached a nearby watercourse, found a canoe, and paddled to a settlement called Fort Stoddard. She was shown into the presence of General Claiborne and told her story of the massacre.

At Fort Mims the final tragedy occurred. When smoke in the loft drove the terrified children to the lower floor, additional flames from fires set in different places outside made life inside unbearable. The choice for the last defenders was to leave the blockhouse, face hundreds of Indians, or stay inside and be burned to death. Adding to the horror of those moments were the howls, taunts, and screams of waiting Indians who danced and waved weapons on this dark night. For the defenders surely it was a scene from hell.

Some ran outside. They were immediately lost in a mêlée of screaming Indians who shot, clubbed, and knifed them to death. Others died in walls of fire as the blockhouse was consumed, screaming, crying, struggling until burning wood fell upon them.

The previous year, 1812, the United States and Great Britain had gone to war for the second time within living memory. But the War of 1812 was for the

4

most part being conducted in the northern and easterly parts of the nation, and while it raged and the White House was burned by the British, hundreds of miles southward, with poor roads and even poorer means of communication, the Fort Mims disaster, while actually a war within a war, had repercussions that resulted in fights that had no bearing on the national war.

What happened at Fort Mims was in the minds of frontiersmen the cause of a war that they would pursue to its bloody finale and that, to them, was known as the Creek War, after the name of the preponderance of fighting Indians, the Creeks, who got their name from the British who said their entire area was criss-crossed with creeks, which was an accurate description.

In a huge territory of the southern part of the nation at that time, settlers and settlements were poorly defended, if at all, something which years of more or less peace between red men and white had encouraged. Intermarriage was common. Indians farmed as did whites; both races supported an economy that was adequate for the times. What caused the Creeks to take up the hatchet was an Eastern Indian named Tecumseh who advocated a great confederation of tribesmen to drive out the whites who had taken lands the Indians claimed. The Creeks did not join Tecumseh's confederation, but his mission among the Creeks and other southern tribes solved seeds of resentment against all whites that inevitably led to the Fort Mims massacre and the Creek War.

Subsequent to the Fort Mims massacre, with the settlements aroused and hastening to muster militia,

5

tales of atrocities spread. Friendly Indians were no longer welcome in the settlements, and people on isolated farms lived in constant fear.

About ten miles from the Tennessee village of Winchester, in a log house surrounded by tillable land close to the banks of Bean Creek, a locally renowned hunter named David Crockett lived with his red-headed wife. She was called Polly, although her real name was Mary. They lived comfortably, if not extravagantly, with their three children: Margaret, William, and John Wesley.

Crockett was in his twenties, slightly over six feet tall, with brown hair and eyes. He was imbued with an insatiable wanderlust that would never leave him. When he heard there was to be a muster of volunteers to fight Indians, he rode to Winchester and volunteered. Afterward he rode home and told Polly what he had done and that the volunteer contingent was to leave that night.

She dutifully prepared a pack for him, and stood in the cabin doorway, watching her man riding to war. He had said in parting he would come back now and then, which probably did little for Polly Crockett's heartache. Now she had full responsibility for their children and their livelihood. His enlistment was for sixty days, not too long a period of time, unless, of course, he never came home, or did so in a canvas bag in the bed of a wagon.

Commanding officer for the area was General Andrew Jackson, an impatient, fiery-tempered man ten years older than David Crockett. He early displayed something just short of contempt for the militia. He commanded the regular Army, of which there were not enough men to conduct a full-scale war over interminable miles of rivers, forests, mountains, and the hordes of fighting tribesmen. By the time he undertook the Army's advance toward Indian country, the Winchester volunteers, who had been joined by other volunteers, had a combined strength of about two thousand men of which the Winchester volunteers accounted for slightly more than half.

They moved into hostile country, crossed out of Tennessee into Alabama at a place call Muscle Shoals, made camp on a ridge that commanded a view of the area, and put scouts out in all directions. This was hostile Indian country and no frontiersman would believe Indian scouts did not know they had crossed the river and how strong they were.

During their wait for the regulars under Jackson, an advance unit rode into camp under Major John H. Gibson, who served under one of Jackson's favorites, Colonel John Coffee.

When Gibson said he wanted some of the best-qualified frontiersmen to scout ahead, he was told the best man was Davy Crockett. The major chose Crockett and asked him to recommend the man to go with him.

Crockett looked the part in his buckskin clothing, moccasins, in his prime at twenty-seven, bearded and muscular. He called up George Russell with whom Crockett had made many scouts.

Major Gibson said Russell was too young; he hadn't even begun to shave, to which an irritated Crockett said that, if whiskers made the man, then billy goats should lead and govern.

The major accepted George Russell. Another ten men were also selected. The following morning, early, the men left camp, well mounted and heavily armed, under the orders of Major Gibson. Later they met, and took with them an Indian trader who volunteered to guide them through a countryside he knew very well.

They were moving through territory even their trader guide was uneasy about when Major Gibson decided to divide the party. He would take half, and Crockett would take the other half. They would make a wide sweep and meet at a crossroads fifteen miles ahead.

From here on the possibility of an ambush was very real. Both parties progressed carefully with outriders on all sides, using every experienced frontiersman's trick of deception not to be discovered.

It was a long, harrowing ride. By dividing the command, the major had assured that if either party had to fight, they could not possibly prevail against the hundreds of Indians who used this territory as a hunting ground. It was to their advantage that they rode at night. That in fact may have been their only advantage before they reached the point of rendezvous the following morning.

Major Gibson was not there, nor did he arrive later in the day, a situation that put Crockett and his companions on a vigilant alert, suspecting as they did that the major and his party may have been ambushed and annihilated.

The anxiety was too much for some of the scouts who told Crockett they were going back. This would further weaken Crockett's party and would, as was pointed out to the would-be defectors, make it highly improbable that they could go back the way they had come without being killed by Indians.

Because Gibson was obviously not going to appear at the rendezvous, Crockett led his small band in the direction of a village of friendly Cherokees some twenty miles distant. On the way they crossed the clearing owned by a white man married to a Creek woman who was clearly worried when the band of heavily armed scouts approached his cabin. He told Crockett that only a short while before ten warriors had visited him, and, if they should return, to find him talking to white scouts, they would all be killed. The man's advice, while perhaps justified, was not followed by Crockett. The squawman said: "Go back where you came from."

Crockett did the opposite. He continued on the trail to the village of friendly Cherokees.

They found the village after dark by its many fires. When they were closer, they could hear Indians calling back and forth. Crockett made a sortie on foot, lay in hiding for some time, and decided the Cherokees were still friendly because in hostile villages a pole painted red was prominently displayed. At this village there was no such pole.

If the Indians were surprised when a party of armed white men rode into their village, they did not show it — for a while anyway.

They fed the scouts, cared for their horses, treated them as friends, but did not appear altogether happy to have them as guests. These Indians were one of the groups that tried hard to maintain a degree of neutrality between the hostiles and the whites. When the Indians decided they had done for the whites what was expected of peaceful and friendly people, a spokesman asked Crockett to leave, which Crockett agreed to do before dawn.

Late in the night, when the camp was totally quiet, a Cherokee went to Crockett's bed ground and whispered the two words guaranteed to awaken Crockett: "Red Sticks."

If it had been a ruse to get rid of the white men, it could not have succeeded better than it did. But it wasn't a ruse. An Indian runner had arrived with news that a great army of hostiles had crossed the Coos River at a place called Ten Islands, moving in the direction of the road the runner said was being used by a large army of regular soldiers marching into Creek territory.

To Crockett that had to mean the Indians, whose moccasin telegraph was better than the white man's method of passing information, knew Jackson was coming, knew by what route, his strength, and were amassing to attack him.

Crockett and his scouts pushed their horses to the very limit to reach Jackson's column. They rode sixty-five miles in twelve hours on horses that had not been properly cared for during the entire period of their enlistment up to this time.

They made that ride through territory infested with hostile warriors without incident and found Colonel Coffee's advance on animals ready to drop. Crockett did this believing the Army was in imminent danger of annihilation as it marched against invisible foemen. He had taken great risks, had pushed his men and animals to the verge of exhaustion, but he had found Coffee's advance force in time.

Colonel Coffee listened to what Crockett had to say, dismissed him, and did nothing toward increasing the size of his advance scouting parties or taking additional precautions.

Crockett was stunned, then he was angered. He went directly to General Jackson where his reception was even chillier, but a little later, when Major Gibson arrived with the other half of Crockett's scouting party, and gave the same report, General Jackson sent eight hundred volunteers under Colonel Coffee to seek the Indians. Crockett's scouts accompanied this force, which was not only large and noisy but which permitted Red Eagle's allies to provide the hostiles with the route of march and the size of Coffee's column.

CHAPTER
TWO

To War And Back

Colonel Coffee's destination was an Indian town called Black Warrior's Village. His purpose was to sweep the countryside and engage any Indians he encountered. Black Warrior's Village was where the city of Tuscaloosa now stands. Crockett and his scouts rode in advance and on both sides of the marching column.

For an excellent reason they found no Indians. Red Eagle had learned enough from other confrontations with the Army to choose his battle grounds.

Coffee's column reached Black Warrior's Village and found it deserted. Because the Army was never adequately supplied, the soldiers ransacked the town, found quantities of grain, corn, and cured meat. They rested there, fed their horses well, and, as they prepared to march deeper into hostile territory, Colonel Coffee ordered the town burned, which was done. When the march was resumed, there was nothing left of Black Warrior's Village but ash and embers.

From this point forward Colonel Coffee directed the march without offering objectives, which bothered Crockett and others. They had reason to doubt the colonel's competency at fighting Indians, something they knew about from experience.

Regardless of Coffee's strength, the party was now in the heart of hostile country. It could be assumed with thousands of Indians throughout this area that Coffee's movements would be watched by day and night.

The anxiety spread to the regular soldiers. The column was riding deep into Creek territory. At any moment it could be attacked by overwhelming numbers of Red Sticks.

After passing through the Chickasaw and Choctaw territories without incident, it began to appear to Davy Crockett that Coffee was leading his Army too deep into a deadly, dangerous countryside where retreat would be impossible if it was attacked from the rear.

The Army marched to Ten Islands on the Coosa River. Here, Colonel Coffee directed that a mud and log fortification be erected. Here, too, Crockett and other scouts fanned out, seeking Indians.

They found a small party of hostiles, surrounded them, and offered them a choice between being shot or surrendering. The leader of this band was an Indian named Bob Catala. He surrendered.

Some six or eight miles distant the scouts found an Indian town — with a red pole. They awaited the arrival of the soldiers. Accompanying Coffee's column now was a party of Cherokees under an Indian, Colonel Dick Brown, whose rank was legitimate. He had earned it in previous battles as an ally of the whites.

Crockett went ahead with his scouts to make sure there were no ambushing warriors on either side of the town. Despite being a heavily timbered area, dangerous for scouting parties, no Indians were encountered.

Colonel Coffee made his disposition, which was to divide the command with each division to move through the forests on either side, and when they met to close the surround. This was accomplished because of the densely overgrown areas around the town.

Coffee then detached a party of rangers to move into plain sight of the town, which they did, and, when the Indians saw them, they charged the white men, yelling and brandishing weapons. The rangers retreated in loose order until they were within musket range of the soldiers in the forest on the near side of the town.

As the rangers rode clear, the soldiers, both kneeling and standing, fired a thunderous volley. For several moments the firing line was obscured by gunsmoke. As it cleared, the soldiers could see dead and dying Indians by the dozen.

The surviving Indians fled back into their town and the soldiers tightened their surround, firing at anything that moved. Later, this would be called the Battle of Tallushatches. Army casualties: five killed and fifteen wounded.

Davy had seen a number of warriors run into a house in whose doorway sat an Indian woman with a bow and arrows. She used her feet to steady the bow, used both hands to draw the gut string, and fired. Her arrow killed an officer named Moore.

At least twenty musket balls hit the woman. She died in the doorway.

Enraged soldiers charged the building, firing as they ran. Some Creeks fired back but with the door open, held in that position by the dead woman, they had limited range.

Soldiers got in close and set the house on fire. Some Indians ran outside where soldiers shot them; others were burned to death. The total number was forty-six Indians killed, including the woman in the doorway.

The town was captured. The dead and wounded Indians numbered one hundred and eighty-six. Women and children became captives.

When it was over, Crockett went hunting. There was not enough food in the Indian town for the soldiers as there had been at Black Warrior's Village, and marching men required food and lots of it.

While Crockett was gone, an Indian arrived who wanted to speak to the commanding officer. Within a few minutes after Coffee and the Indian conferred, orders were issued to set the column in motion for another advance.

This order was not appreciated. The men had been marching for days with insufficient food. Their shoes were wearing out; their clothing was filthy and torn; they had not profited at all at the latest Indian town. Demoralization inevitably set in, and, while they were in the very heartland of hostile Creek country, desertions occurred.

The route of march was from the Tallushatches town across the Coosa River in the general direction of a place called Talladega, where Jackson's element of the divided command was to meet Coffee's party.

Men were gaunt and tired, some had injuries, all were unwashed and unshaven. They had been unable to sleep, eat, or even to rest.

Davy Crockett's horse, Jeb, was wearing out; all the horses were. An occasional hatful of corn was far less than was required to maintain horses in constant use.

Davy hunted ahead of the marchers. He, too, was haggard, stained, and gaunt.

Where the rendezvous with Jackson was accomplished, the general directed that a fortification be erected. When it was completed, it was called Fort Strother. This was in the Ten Islands vicinity of the Coosa River.

Jackson's policy was to have fortifications available in his rear in the event a retreat became necessary.

Jackson could not move until his Army had been provisioned, an enterprise that throughout his campaign against the Creeks was at best tardy and wholly inadequate. He fumed, his Army waited, and Davy Crockett hunted as did others. Through this source some food was provided but not enough.

Here, Crockett had an interesting encounter with an Indian who paddled his canoe to the bank where Crockett was concealed. When the Indian beached his canoe, Crockett came into view, rifle in the crook of one arm. The Indian seemed to have taken root. Crockett asked if the Indian had any corn. The Indian did have some. Crockett offered him a silver coin. The Indian was unimpressed. He asked if Crockett had bullets. He offered to trade corn for ammunition. The trade was made, two hatfuls of corn for ten bullets and ten loads of powder.

The appeals of an Indian from Talladega for General Jackson to march to the support of friendlies forted up with hundreds of Red Sticks besieging them at Talladega resulted in an order for the Army to march.

Among Jackson's soldiers the principal reason they marched was the hope that Fort Talladega would be amply provisioned.

Jackson's command was a motley one, ragged, gaunt, and unshaven regulars, marching with undisciplined allied Indians of different clans and tribes and militiamen clad in whatever attire they chose. Horsemen rode scarecrow mounts, and because this was malaria country, the general's sick list increased daily.

Jackson's troops had to take the fort. They were too near starvation — and destitution — to do otherwise.

Crockett scouted in advance of the marching column. When he arrived in the vicinity of Fort Talladega, he got the shock of his life. There were no less than eleven hundred Red Sticks camped around the fort. More Indians in one bunch than he had ever seen before, and of course they knew Jackson's Army was coming.

This was December. The ground was muddy, which made marching difficult even for strong, healthy men. For Jackson's host it was torture. Significantly, for wheeled vehicles of any kind, but particularly heavily burdened supply wagon trains, roads were impassable.

The Indians outside the fort tried to entice the Indians inside to come out and join in the attack on Jackson's Army. They told the forted-up Indians

Jackson's command had many fine horses, guns enough for everyone, powder, lead, swords, and knives, good blankets, all of which they would share with the forted-up Indians if they would join the Red Sticks in the battle to come. The friendlies inside the fort said they would hold a council and decide, which they did not do and had no intention of doing. They knew the Army was close. Nevertheless, when the hostiles became increasingly agitated as the Army drew near, the forted-up Indians finally agreed to come out and fight Jackson as allies of the Red Sticks, but only when the Army appeared. This was to be their last desperate attempt to avoid joining the hostiles.

Davy Crockett was returning to the command when he met a friendly who offered to guide the Army through the dense woodlands to the fort.

The weather was chilly. There were dark clouds overhead. The ground was muddy from recent rains, and men bringing up the rear had a disorderly band of prisoners ahead of them. Friendlies trudged along, men, women, and children. These people in particular had reason to fear the Red Sticks, the Creek fighting men who painted themselves from head to heel with red ocher.

Crockett rode ahead, warily now because shouts and screams could be heard ahead. Several of his scouting unit rode with him.

No one doubted that this time there would be a big battle and fierce resistance. Red Eagle had been mustering his forces for many days. He had encouraged the whites to penetrate so deeply into Creek country that they would be unable to be provisioned or retreat.

General Jackson used the same strategy Colonel Coffee had used at Tallushatches. By utilizing friendlies familiar with the area, he divided his command to effect a surround, which he could never have accomplished if there had been ambushing Red Sticks farther out through the forested countryside, but there were no such ambushers, probably because Red Eagle wanted all his fighting men in one place after he knew Jackson was getting close.

The forted-up Indians had a good view from their parapets. They could see what was happening, which the Red Sticks outside the fort could not. They nevertheless were not without their own variety of strategy. Hundreds of them hid below a creekbank where only the friendlies on their catwalk could see them.

Jackson's men used up a lot of time slipping far out and around the fort on both sides. When the surround was completed, Major Russell, the father of Davy Crockett's scouting companion, George Russell, was sent ahead to bring on the action.

As he advanced, the Indians on the catwalks began shouting and gesticulating. Major Russell was leading his party directly toward the cutbank where those hundreds of hidden warriors were waiting.

What prevented a disaster was that several Indians jumped to the ground, ran forward, grabbed the major's horse by the bit, and turned it back.

Finally understanding what all the shouting and gesticulating had been about, the major halted, then began to turn back with his companions.

Indians came from beneath the cutbank, shouting and firing muskets and arrows. Russell's men abandoned their horses and raced for the protection of the fort.

When the Indians left the protection of the cutbank and charged, their companions joined in a general mêlée. Hundreds of them charged toward an area where soldiers were not visible.

The same thing happened at Talladega as had happened at Tallushatches. The soldiers held their fire until the Indians were close, then volley-fired, a kneeling rank firing with time to reload as the standing rank behind them fired.

The carnage was unbelievable. The Indians reversed their charge and, possibly, with some idea of escaping, charged into the withering gunfire of the other division of Jackson's force.

This time survivors did not run except as far as the nearest cover. They were armed with a variety of weapons, bows and arrows, old smooth-bore muskets, even hand weapons, but their most formidable weapon was the bow. An accomplished bowman could keep five arrows in the air at a time while a warrior with an old musket required much more time to get his weapon loaded, charged, and ready to fire.

The noise was deafening. Indians shouted, gunfire was constant, clouds of burned powder made targeting difficult. The forted-up Indians howled, jumped, and waved their arms.

Finally the surviving Red Sticks came together and made a desperate charge against the center of Jackson's line, which was being held by the militia. The volunteers fired their weapons empty, then ran in all directions. The Indians got out of the surround in this fashion and escaped — but not many of them.

The Battle of Talladega cost Jackson's Army fifteen men killed during the fighting and two who died later of wounds. Indian losses, according to Davy Crockett, were "upward of four hundred."

The command rested at the fort for several days, and because no provisions had arrived before the battle, the victors depleted the fort's stores, and, as hunger increased, scouts were sent to locate the wagons supposedly on their way. They found no wagons.

When this became known, there was talk of mutiny. It did not help that the weather turned cold and the horses were becoming weaker by the day.

Several officers went to General Jackson for permission to allow the sixty-day volunteers — who had already served long past that time — to go home, get fresh animals, winter clothing, food, and return.

Jackson refused. He had no illusions about those men returning.

Davy Crockett was a leader among the near-mutineers who were determined to leave regardless of the general's order. In order to leave the volunteers had to cross a bridge. Jackson had a cannon, some regulars and militiamen stationed on the opposite side of the bridge.

Crockett led the dissenters onto the bridge and started across it. Midway, with rifles primed and ready, the men advanced. On the opposite side of the bridge the regulars cocked their weapons. Crockett's men did the same and continued across. Anything could have caused a tragedy, but nothing did. The only sound was of men crossing a wooden bridge. When they were about to leave the bridge, the regulars yielded ground, and Crockett's party was joined by some of the opposing militiamen.

Andrew Jackson's blistering anger at the men who had not only allowed the defectors to pass but had in some cases joined them resulted in an order that the men who had suffered so much and who had fought so valiantly was arbitrarily to extend their enlistment six months and his calling them the damnedest volunteers he had ever seen in his life.

It was a petulant gesture since the general did not expect the volunteers to return, and in fact many did not return.

On their way home the defectors met a regiment of other sixty-day volunteers on their way to join the Army at Talladega. This encounter was in the vicinity of Huntsville.

Otherwise, as the ragged, gaunt frontiersmen on their leg-weary, half-starved mounts rode homeward in the midst of a countryside in fear and turmoil because hostile, vengeful Indians burned, murdered, and plundered indiscriminately, riding at will, attacking suddenly, and yet escaped the best efforts of settler bands to find them.

The closer they got to Winchester, individual volunteers and small parties of them left the main group, heading for their homes.

When Davy was passing through a wild, uninhabited area of forests and creeks, his horse twice raised its head to look backward. The first time it did this, Davy paid no attention. In primeval forests there were always strange scents, but the second time the horse did it, Davy changed course, rode into the timber and underbrush, dismounted, and watched his back trail.

Two painted warriors, one with roached hair, were tracking him.

He stood with one hand poised to clamp down on the horse's nostrils in case it attempted to nicker or move.

Once the Indians paused to study tracks and confer. Both had muskets, and carried ammunition pouches, knives, and tomahawks. Both were painted for war.

Davy watched them confer where his tracks abruptly turned in the direction of his hiding place. While they were stationary, Davy rested the barrel of his rifle in the crotch of a tree and aimed. As the warriors broke off talking and looked in the direction the tracks would lead them, Davy fired. One warrior dropped in his tracks. The other one sprinted toward the forest on Davy's left.

He hastily lowered the rifle to reload, was tamping in the charge when the surviving warrior charged with his tomahawk held aloft. His timing was excellent.

Crockett was still tamping in his charge when the Indian ran toward him.

Davy had no time to remove the ramrod. He barely had time to raise the gun and cock it. The Indian was large and muscular. When Davy fired, the warrior was close. The ramrod pierced the Indian. It would probably have exited in back if it hadn't struck the breastbone.

Momentum carried the Indian to within five feet of Crockett. This was the warrior with the roached hair, which normally would have made a fine trophy, but Davy had another concern. The noise of gunshots would certainly bring other hostiles. He reloaded, listened, and watched. Eventually satisfied his victims were a pair of coursing Indians unaccompanied by comrades, he left the Indians where they lay and continued on toward home.

CHAPTER
THREE

One War Ends

Davy's wife and children were delighted to see him crossing the clearing toward the cabin on an exhausted horse, soiled, stained, and gaunt.

While he rested, gained some lost weight, was cared for by his wife, and played with the children, news of sporadic Indian attacks, killings, burnings, and ambushes reached him, as it also reached all frontier settlements and outlying homesteads. While Davy enjoyed his respite from events and persons he did not much care for besides General Jackson, he was aware of the dearth of provisions for the soldiers and horses. He was convinced that the war would not end soon, so he reenlisted.

During his absence from the fighting there had been changes. General Jackson and most of his army had been ordered southward where the British, in addition to supplying the Indians with arms, appeared to have some plan of carrying their war with the United States as far south as the settlements in the Louisiana country.

Left in command after Jackson's departure was Colonel Coffee who pushed as far into hostile territory as the Tallapposa River. It was January; the weather was unpleasant. Both wars, the Creek War and the War of

1812 between the United States and Great Britain had now been in progress two years. Coffee's contingent of the divided command consisted of about eight hundred men, including allied tribesmen and volunteers.

At a place called Horseshoe Bend, because the river turned back on itself, Davy, accompanied by allied Indians and old friends of Major Russell's rangers, found fresh and abundant sign of hostiles in large numbers. When the scouts returned, Crockett reported what had been found and the number of guards was increased. The bivouac was in a swale surrounded by forests.

The arrival of provisions from Mobile put the command in high spirits. Some spirits were unusually high since the supplies included cases of whiskey.

After so much hardship the soldiers rested, ate well, recovered some of their earlier enthusiasm, eventually bedded down near the fires to offset the cold, and slept like the dead until a couple of hours before dawn when musket fire awakened them. The guards ran back, shouting the alarm. Men were instantly alerted. Wood was heaped on dying fires to provide light for riflemen to see the attacking Indians, but at Talladega as well as through other encounters the Indians had learned their lessons well. They did not charge into the firelight but remained hidden. Both sides had little more than muzzle blasts as targets. Russell's men used every bit of cover they could find. As appeared to be customary with Red Sticks, this fight ended about dawn when the Indians abruptly withdrew, carrying their casualties with them. This engagement cost the command four dead and about a dozen wounded.

The withdrawal of this force was undertaken after the dead were buried where they had fallen, and horse-drawn travois were constructed to transport the wounded. Every yard of the retreat was observed by Indians.

Crockett and the other scouts covered the sides and the rear. They found no Indians.

When the command came to Enotachapco Creek, which was running high, and after about half the command reached the far shore, the Indians attacked. Their particular targets were the artillerymen. Davy Crockett with other scouts who had been in the rear covering the retreat arrived on lathered horses with a party of howling Creeks chasing them.

At the height of this fight two officers deserted, crossed the river below the area of combat, and were not seen again. They had evidently judged the action correctly. The Army could not withdraw and could not finish crossing the creek. The Indians who had chased Russell's scouts had been reinforced. They not only had the initiative but the divided command could neither unify nor retreat.

Later Davy said because gunners were being shot as they tried to man their guns and the Indians were in great numbers on both sides of the creek, there was no other alternative than to fight as long as it was possible. He and other men in buckskin dug in and sniped. Anyone standing erect did not survive.

This Battle of Enotachapco Creek was fought in late January of 1814. It ended with one of those bizarre abrupt Indian withdrawals.

A unique factor in this engagement undoubtedly encouraged the victorious Indians to break off the fight. That occurred when Crockett's band of scouts manned one six-pound cannon with devastating effect.

Casualties at Enotachapco were twenty volunteers killed and seventy-five wounded. This time the Indians did not carry off their dead, which numbered one hundred and eighty-nine.

Indian casualties were so high they were rarely afterward capable of mounting massive attacks. In fact, before Jackson's withdrawal southward, he fought and won the final large battle of the Creek War. This conflict occurred at Horseshoe Bend where the Indians had created a massive log and earthen rampart. In this fight Red Eagle commanded the Red Sticks. He had been accumulating a force of Indians for some time. His fortification was strong, capably manned by more than a thousand Indians, and was amply provisioned. Jackson's force consisted of three thousand troops with artillery. That large a force could not elude detection nor did it. Jackson's force arrived before the fortifications in March, 1814, a few weeks after the Battle of Enotachapco and while the general had been in the process of beginning his march toward New Orleans. He had reason to get the Creek War over quickly. Jackson despised the British and wished nothing more than to fight them.

Nevertheless, his preparations at Horseshoe Bend showed no evidence of haste. Jackson's first move after the two warring parties faced each other was to offer sanctuary to women and children, which the Indians accepted. Then on March 27th the attack began, and, while it lasted, the fighting, noise, and smoke created an atmosphere no witnesses would ever forget.

The Indians had only bows and arrows and small arms. They fought like tigers and were nearly obliterated. Before the fighting subsided, between eight hundred and nine hundred Indians had been killed. Five hundred women and children survived in captivity.

Red Eagle's loss was fatal to his cause although he personally survived. General Jackson said: "The carnage was terrible." Casualties for the United States were fifty-one killed and one hundred and forty-eight wounded.

So the Creek War was effectively ended at Horseshoe Bend although separate and individual skirmishes, ambushes, and snipings would continue. The reason for this was simple. The peace treaty of August, 1814, had the hostiles agree to cede their country and withdraw from the southern and western parts of what became in 1819 the State of Alabama. However, the southern Creeks had not been part of the negotiations nor had they agreed to, much less signed, the treaty. They had been and remained absolutely opposed to any ceding of Indian land.

Notwithstanding, General Jackson could consider his interior lines secure after Red Eagle's defeat. The staggering Indian losses made it clear they would never again be able to meet invaders in large numbers. Jackson was now free to march into Louisiana where he brushed aside skirmishers and routed a meager Spanish garrison, declared martial law, had his command reinforced by volunteers from Kentucky and Tennessee, and was prepared to give battle by mid-December, 1814.

His Army consisted of about five thousand men. After several probing tests of strength, the British commander, Sir Edward Packenham, advanced his force of eight thousand men at dawn on January 8, 1814, in close order against Jackson's earthworks of which cotton bales formed a considerable bulwark. This battle, called by Americans the Second War of Independence, employed the identical tactic of the original War of Independence. General Packenham sent his veterans of the Napoleonic War in tight formation, shoulder to shoulder, against Jackson's force of marksmen protected by hastily erected, crude but excellent fortifications.

Packenham's army was cut to pieces. British losses were three hundred killed, twelve hundred and fifty wounded, and five hundred captured. American losses were fourteen killed, thirty-nine wounded, and eighteen captured. Jackson's triumph was called the most astounding victory of the war.

It emphasized something else — the abysmal lack of communication between the northern part of the country and the southern part. On December 24, 1814, a peace treaty had been signed at Ghent in Belgium, ending the war. The Battle of New Orleans was fought two weeks after the war had officially ended.

However, while Andrew Jackson was a national hero and would become the seventh President of the United States and the British were gone, the Creeks, Cherokees, and their allies, especially those who opposed and defied Red Eagle's peace after his resounding defeat at Horseshoe Bend, remained hostile to whites.

Unrelenting and sporadic fighting continued. The untamed wildernesses of Tennessee, Alabama, and their environs reinforced Kentucky's colloquial name among frontiersmen as "the dark and bloody ground."

In Davy Crockett's part of the country the change was in many ways worse than it had been when Indian armies numbering in the thousands fought pitched battles with the whites. Now, the fighting was unpredictable, attacks were by stealth, ambushers left dead victims and vanished without a sign.

At this time a tragedy struck Davy Crockett from which he would never completely recover. His wife Polly fell ill and died of malaria, leaving Davy with three young children, the youngest a baby. His youngest brother who was married with children of his own moved to the Crockett cabin, and Davy at least had a woman in the house to care for his youngsters.

It was a time in his life he would be unable to handle very well. He knew death first-hand but this kind of death, of Polly, his red-headed wife, the love of his life, left him desolate, and the care of his children, while a solace of sorts, could do nothing about the grief and loneliness.

He was thirty-two years old when he erected a cairn of stones over Polly's grave. He hunted, farmed a little, visited the pond where he and Polly had bathed, and had afterward dried in the sun.

Even with the help of his brother and his sister-in-law with children of their own the cabin was still too full of memories. He took his children and moved west, to Shoal Creek, near the farm of a war widow named Elizabeth Patton who had two children. Davy had known her husband. They had fought together at Tallushatches. In time he decided for his own sake as well as for the sake of his children he would re-marry. Davy went about his courtship, it was said, as sly about it as a fox when he is going to rob a hen roost.

Once David Crockett and Elizabeth Patton were married, they had five children between them. Over the years they had children of their own. When the youngsters got into a fight, Davy would call to Bess: "Your children and my children are whipping hell out of our children."

It was a good union, but as time passed newcomers in wagons arrived to select land and build cabins, something Davy was not unaccustomed to. His old restlessness returned. He decided to explore a tract of land the government had recently obtained from the Chickasaw Indians. He left home with three friends to explore this new land. One companion was bitten by a water moccasin and was left with a friendly farm family while Crockett and his remaining two friends went on their way.

They reached the Chickasaw country and found that, although the government had deed to the area, not many Indians were willing to leave territory they had lived in for hundreds of years. Nor was it just the Chickasaws. Unregenerate Creeks and Cherokees also lived in this primitive country. For the latter two bands of tribesmen the appearance of white men was reason for hostility.

Davy and his friends were experienced frontiersmen. They rightfully assumed from the sullenness of the Indians that regardless of a piece of paper that transferred title of their territory to the whites this was their ancient homeland and trespassers — whites or others — were not welcome. This was made clear in an unusual way.

Davy began to run a fever. Whatever the cause — probably malaria — within a few days he was too ill to travel, nor did it help that the saddle animals ran off, heading for home, and were not recovered.

He was lying beside the trail, perspiring heavily, shaking and hot to the touch when a pair of Indians appeared. They offered to help him to the nearby cabin of a man named Jones. Because the distance was about a mile and Davy could barely walk, one Indian carried his rifle and his companion supported Davy until they reached the Jones cabin. Here, the Indians, who were hunters, left, and Jesse Jones, a reclusive frontiersman who also wore buckskin trousers and hunting shirt, cared for Davy, who had bouts of high fever and delirium.

Recovery was slow and time-consuming. During his period of recuperation, Davy and Jesse Jones would sit on the cabin's porch, smoking their pipes and talking. They had much in common — both had fought in the Indian wars, both were great storytellers, both had a sly sense of humor, and had lived by hunting most of their adult lives.

One afternoon an Indian friend of Jones's came by the cabin to say a band of horseback soldiers were coming. Davy asked how many. All the Indian could do was make the *wibluta* sign for "many." He also said they were coming to find and take away some Indians accused of murdering whites and stealing horses.

After the Indian had hurried on toward his village, Jesse Jones told Davy he had heard of the killings some time before and knew for a fact the Indians the soldiers were coming for had not murdered the people nor stolen their horses.

"Senecas did it," he said, renegade Indians from up north. He had been visited by them on their way northward. They had taken his provisions and his horse, but had spared his life. They had the branded horses and considerable plunder including white men's coats, hats, even a parasol along with rifles and pistols.

Davy asked how far the Indian village was.

Jones raised an arm, gesturing easterly. "Six, eight miles."

Davy was briefly silent, then because he knew what soldiers did to Indian villages, he told Jesse Jones the Indians should be warned.

He and Jesse Jones struck out. The older man was unsure about Davy's being able to cover the distance. The countryside was overgrown, mountainous with treacherous footing. Davy was not entirely recovered from his illness, but, if he was nothing else, he was resilient, tough as a boiled owl, and determined. Never during his lifetime did anything as exasperating as illness prevent him from doing things he was convinced should be done.

The Indian messenger who had stopped by the Jones cabin had already reached the village, which was in turmoil. By the time Davy and his companion reached it, preparations were being made to abandon the village and take to the forest.

Jesse Jones leaned on his rifle, watching the excitement, and shook his head as he spoke to Davy. "They'll abandon their hogs 'n' chickens, their cattle, their stores of grain. You know what the soldiers'll do, don't you?"

Davy knew. "Kill the animals, eat what they want, leave the rest dead, then burn the settlement. You sure these Indians had nothing to do with the raid you told me about?"

"Dead certain for a blessed fact. I know redskins as well as you do. They was Senecas from Pennsylvania. I grew to manhood in their country." Jesse almost smiled at Davy. "I expect the reason they didn't kill me was because I knew their language."

For a moment Jesse Jones was quiet, then he added: "A hunnert scairt Indians with squaws an' pups an' two white skins. The Army'll make a massacre and, unless we step lively, we'll be part of it. Soldiers just naturally shoot anyone wearin' moccasins. Davy, it's time we leave. Nothin' can stop what's goin' to happen."

Davy left Jones to his fatalistic ruminations, sought the agitated spokesman for the Indians, and told him there might be a way to avoid a massacre.

The Indian considered Davy in stoic silence until a powerfully built, large half-breed spoke rapidly and forcefully to the spokesman, who turned to the big half-breed and those around him and spoke to them in a harsh voice. He then asked Davy what could be done.

Davy spoke bluntly. "Stop the preparations to leave. Make your people go back to their cabins. Tell them to act like they don't know the soldiers are coming. Tell them to act like nothing is wrong. Tell the bucks to leave their guns inside."

A surly, very dark Indian said: "That will make it easier for the soldiers to kill us."

Davy had a ready answer to that. "They'll kill you anyway. If you run, they'll hunt you down like rats . . . women, children, old people, and warriors. If you pretend not to know they are coming, if you do not offer to fight them, it might not be a massacre. If they come shooting, then we fight them."

The surly dark man's eyes widened. "We? You fight with us?"

Davy nodded.

The spokesman sent the dark man to tell the others they were not to flee; they were to do as the white scout said. It was the spokesman's order.

Davy returned to Jesse Jones, told him what he had done, and Jones eyed Davy with strong skepticism. "You know how they do it? Make a sneaky big surround an', when everything's ready, they charge the village, shootin' and yellin'."

Davy took Jones back where the spokesman and other Indians stood. The entire group watched the surly, dark man and his companions trying mightily to reverse the preparations for flight. In many instances they had to use force and even then people hesitated before obediently going to their cabins, but not all the warriors left their weapons out of sight.

The Indian who had brought the message after stopping at the Jones place approached Davy. Like the other Indians, after a hundred years of living near whites, he spoke passable English. He said: "If soldiers shoot, we will tear you apart and trample your guts."

CHAPTER
FOUR

Trespassing

Jesse Jones volunteered to scout for soldiers. He took the large half-breed with him and the surly, dark Indian.

Davy remained with the spokesman whose councilors hovered. Davy lighted his pipe. The Indians tried hard to follow Davy's example of unconcern. The people also did their best to appear normal at their chores. A close inspection would certainly have detected the stiffness, the unnatural quiet, the repetitive work of women and men, but Davy was satisfied that in general and from the distance of the surrounding forest the appearance of normality would be convincing.

The dark, surly Indian returned shining with sweat and troubled. Jesse Jones had sent him to warn that the mounted soldiers were less than a mile westward.

Davy sent the news bearer back to Jones. The Indians counseled in their own language, of which Davy understood enough to know that they were unwilling to risk the lives of their women and children. He spoke English to the spokesman, who listened but not without an expression of apprehension. He was, however, committed to Crockett's scheme and told his tribesmen it was too late to do otherwise than sit, wait, and act normal.

The second time a messenger came from Jesse Jones it was the large half-breed Indian. He said the soldiers had scouts out. Jesse wanted to know if Davy wanted captives. Davy did and sent the big Indian back to say he not only wanted captives but preferably white ones.

He knocked his little pipe empty with the Indians around watching everything he did. He later confided to Bess that a man couldn't get any closer "to shaking hands with God" than he had on that particular day.

Jesse Jones came into the clearing with his two companions and three soldiers who had been detailed to mind the horses after the soldiers dismounted to prepare their surround. All of the captives were white but there was a distinction. Two of the captives were enlisted men; the third man was a lieutenant. His name was Rufus Lee. He had been detached from the 39th company of mounted infantry. He was a raw-boned, lanky man, tanned and weathered, clearly an old campaigner.

When he saw Davy sitting with the Indian leader, his expression of defiance changed. When he and his companions were halted and told by Jesse to sit on the ground, Lee addressed Davy Crockett. "Do you remember me from Black Warrior's Village? I remember you real well."

Davy did not remember the officer but nodded as he said: "Who's commanding your soldiers?"

Lee's gaze did not leave Crockett's face when he replied. "Captain Sam Houston. Do you remember him? He did right proud at Horseshoe Bend."

Davy remembered Houston. What he remembered was that Houston, a large, shaggy-headed man, fought like a tiger and gave no quarter.

Davy arose, left the others briefly to talk to Jesse Jones, then returned, sat down, and asked Lieutenant Lee how many soldiers were out there. Lee answered without hesitation. "Sixty-five. No volunteers."

One of the councilors spoke in his own language to the spokesman whose only reaction, indicating he had understood, was to sit straighter and regard Rufus Lee from unblinking black eyes.

Davy ignored this minor distraction and again addressed the lieutenant. "Where did you come from?"

"Back near Talladega. We was to wait there in case the Red Sticks got cranky about the new country bein' opened up. We was to make a sweep if there was trouble."

Davy gestured. "You call this trouble?"

"No. We didn't know this place was here. Our orders was to scour around after some settlers was attacked in their wagons southeast of Talladega. Our scouts stumbled onto this place."

The lieutenant twisted to glance around. Warriors stood outside cabins, mostly with guns, women pounded roots, scraped hides, yelled at children. He faced back with a quizzical look. "You knew we was coming?"

Davy nodded. Lieutenant Lee was obviously sufficiently knowledgeable about Indians to recognize the forced normality around him. He scowled slightly as he again addressed Davy. "You got Red Sticks hid in the forest?"

Davy's attention was caught by a small party of men approaching. Jesse Jones and his two bucks had two more captives. When he forced them to sit on the ground, Jones said: "Three run for it, but we got these two."

Davy answered with two words. "The horses?"

"They run back the way they come."

"All of them?"

"All but three. One for me, one each for the Indians that was with me."

Davy said: "Burn the saddles, bridles, everything but weapons and food. Fetch them back here."

Jones walked away with his same two companions. Lieutenant Lee, who had heard everything, said: "The men . . . Captain Houston an' the men."

Davy's reply was short. "By now they'll have the surround in place." He unwound up to his full height, leaned on his rifle, and said: "You 'n' me'll walk out in front and you'll call to Houston that your horses are gone. Tell him the Indians'll talk if he's of a mind. Otherwise, they'll kill you 'n' the others."

Lee walked with Davy until they were in the open, then Davy said — "Yell to him." — and Lieutenant Lee did, repeating almost word for word what he had been told.

For a long time there was silence. During this period the lieutenant told Davy that he had served with Houston in other places and that he knew Houston as a man who neither gave quarter nor expected to receive it.

Davy was beginning to worry when an Indian in stained buckskin and moccasins appeared out of the forest with a rifle in the bend of one arm. He stopped, considered Davy, the lieutenant, and the motionless councilmen with their spokesman, then called his answer to Davy's statement.

"You come here."

Davy answered curtly. "You tell Cap'n Houston he needs to talk to me. I don't need to talk to him. So he comes here."

The Indian again stood in long silence. Lee said: "Someone's behind him, tellin' him what to say."

The Indian called again. "Halfway. You come halfway!"

Davy refused. "We talk where I am standing. I wait. Too much talk and you'll lose some soldiers."

A lean, tall man came from the trees, ignored the Indian, and walked purposefully toward Davy. He had a strong jaw, a bold step, and without a hat showed an awry mass of uncut hair. He had a sword at his side and one pistol in his waistband. He needed a shave and his clothing was rumpled and stained. Where he halted, about fifteen feet from Crockett, Sam Houston did not blink an eye as he said: "I thought I recognized you. Have you went an' turned renegade?"

Davy ignored the question. He gestured. "There's fighting Indians in every cabin. There's others where you can't see 'em. If I raise my arm, you 'n' our captives will be shot."

If Houston was impressed, it did not show. He spoke bluntly. "What do you want?"

Davy half turned in the direction of the spokesman, his councilors, and the captives whose backs were to him. He called to them: "Face around!"

When the seated captives obeyed, Captain Houston jumped his stare to the lieutenant who did not say a word, but simply nodded his head.

Houston had recognized the horse guarding detail. Lee's nod answered Houston's unasked questions; their horses had been set free and run off.

Davy did not wait for the anger he knew would be coming. He said: "Them Indians who killed settlers and took their livestock were Senecas . . . not no local Indians. These here is friendlies."

Houston's retort was brusque. "A good Indian is a dead Indian."

Davy did not argue. He said: "You got a long walk, Captain. Soldiers on foot in these forests are like roosting pigeons. If you give the signal for this place to be attacked, I give you my word, there won't be a single soldier, you included, get back to Talladega." Before the red-faced, shaggy-headed man could speak, Davy also said: "Go back. Don't attack no Indian you come onto. Just go back. This here is Indian land. They lived here for . . ."

"This here Indian land was sold to the government!" exclaimed Houston. "They got no right here. It's open for settlement." He glared at Davy. "All right, we'll go back, but, Crockett, it ain't finished. These Indians got to move."

"Where, Captain?"

"How'n hell would I know? My job is to make 'em behave an' that's what I do."

Davy turned slowly in the direction of the forest from which Houston had come. He also looked westerly, then he said: "Just one gunshot, Captain, and they'll trail you all the way back to Talladega, picking men off one at a time until there won't be none of you reach Talladega."

Sam Houston looked long and hard at Crockett before saying: "How can you fight against 'em one time an' fight with 'em the next time? Crockett, I never would have believed it . . . you're a damned renegade."

Davy said nothing. When Houston started back the way he had come, Lieutenant Lee would have followed him, if Davy hadn't caught the officer by the arm and yanked him back. They stood together, watching Captain Houston until he disappeared into the yonder forest, then Davy returned to the council with Rufus Lee, explained what had been accomplished, and told the prisoners, including the officer, that, if they were praying men, now might be a real good time to pray, because if Houston did not keep his word and attacked, they would be the first to be killed.

Jesse Jones and the dark, sulky Indian disappeared into the westerly forest. They did not return for several hours. Houston was keeping his word. Jesse and his companion had watched the unhorsed horse soldiers trudging in unhappy silence back the way they had come. The only time they stopped was when they found the place where their horse equipment, blankets, and saddlebags had been destroyed by fire.

Beyond that point their demoralization was complete. After several miles had been covered, Houston wanted his Indian scouts to abandon their rear-guard position and go ahead of the command.

There were no Indian scouts. Something like sixty-five sullenly angry horse soldiers on foot, who did not care much for Indians anyway, would be likely to take out their anger on any Indian they saw.

They had a long way to go through some of the ruggedest country most of them had ever seen. They had not fought a single Indian. In fact the situation had been reversed; they had been beaten and went blundering their way through a primeval countryside like whipped curs with their tails between their legs.

For Davy the triumph was a mixed blessing. Several days later he fell ill of the same debilitating fever from which he had previously recovered at the cabin of Jesse Jones.

Before it got so bad he couldn't move, he and Jesse left the Indian village on their way back to Jones's cabin.

For Jones it was a harrowing trip. Davy had periods of irrationality, other periods when he would lie down and refuse to get up. But they eventually reached the cabin, and Jesse Jones got a surprise. After putting

Davy to bed, he went outside in the late afternoon and found a horse in the log pen behind his house.

It was the horse he had decided to keep when he, the big Indian, and the dark sulky one had selected animals for themselves before stampeding the Army's animals.

He went to lean on the topmost pole stringer looking at the horse. He eventually slowly turned and studied the area as far as his clearing went and beyond where the forest began. There was no sign of either the dark Indian or the big one, but the only way they could have brought the horse to his clearing and penned it before he and Davy got back was if they had traveled the same route, which could mean they had been sent by their spokesman to make sure Jesse and Davy got safely back to the house.

Three days later when Davy could sit up without breaking into a drenching sweat, Jesse told him about the horse. A week later when Davy felt strong enough to start for home, Jesse offered him the horse. Davy refused, struck out, and walked two days before finding a road. He sat with his back to a rough-barked big tree, placed his rifle across his lap, and rummaged in the parfleche pouch suspended from one shoulder by a thong, brought forth almost the last of the food Jesse Jones had given him, and waited.

It was a long wait. Because the danger of Indian ambushes prevented everything except large parties of heavily armed travelers from using the roads, Davy did not encounter anyone until the morning of the third day when a solitary traveler on the seat of a faded green wagon came along.

He was transporting freight between settlements, took Davy aboard, and explained why he did not fear Indians. His wife was a sister of Red Eagle. They had six children, evenly divided between three girls and three boys. His name was Amos Yardley. He was a gnome of a man, old and bent with stained teeth, sharp eyes, and a tongue that was hinged in the middle and wagged at both ends.

Among the things he told Davy was coming around a bend and meeting seated soldiers on both sides of the road with their shoes off to ease the pain of blisters.

They were unfriendly so he did not stop. He also told Davy of a tavern a few miles ahead where they could bed down in the loft for 6¢ a night, get fed for 10¢, and belly-up to the bar. Drinks were 5¢.

Davy had three silver dollars, one of which had been drilled through, perhaps by an Indian to make a necklace ornament, or by a white man to make a spur rowel.

He and Amos Yardley stopped at the tavern. They were the only visitors who had come from the north, but there were several others, teamsters and travelers who had arrived from the south and the west.

Davy ate, bedded down in the loft, and, when Amos Yardley climbed up also to bed down and brought a bottle of pop-skull, Davy was beginning to feel poorly again and declined the offer as Yardley held the bottle out.

In the morning after a hot breakfast, he left Amos Yardley and struck out on foot. It was no great distance to his home, something like thirty miles, a distance a man of Crockett's build and stamina could make in one day, but not this day. The fever caught him near a lively small creek where he snared three fish, built a cooking fire, ate, drank water, and slept.

The following morning to his surprise, he felt well. It was not far to his cabin but he took his time. The forest was thick, the undergrowth was tangled, and probably because he moved silently, when he moved around a large tree, he met a large brown bear. The animal was as surprised as Davy was.

He raised his rifle and waited. He had no use for bear meat, which he did not feel strong enough to carry, so he let the bear have the initiative.

The big animal had a purple snout from eating berries. It rocked slightly from side to side, evidently trying to make up its mind whether to attack or withdraw.

Davy rested the gun barrel across a low limb, cocked it, and said: "You blue-nosed old son-of-a-bitch, spit or close the winder."

The bear made its decision. It turned and went on its pigeon-toed way making a noise that sounded like a cross between a whine and a growl.

Davy allowed sufficient time to pass for the animal to be out of the area then resumed walking, but for several miles he watched in all directions. From considerable experience he knew that, if there was an unpredictable animal on earth, it was a bear. They had been known to stalk a victim for miles before deciding to attack. He also knew that if any animal, two-legged or four-legged, entered an area that had been marked by a bear, that intruder would be attacked, but the farther he went the more convinced he became that the brown bear had been out foraging and had not been in his marked territory.

When he reached the clearing and started across it, his face was so pale, and so much reduced, that it looked like it had been half soled with brown paper.

Elizabeth was in the cabin doorway, so stiff with shock and disbelief she could not move. Months earlier, when the men he had originally left with returned with his horse, Davy's wife and others believed he was dead. One of those earlier companions said he had helped bury Davy.

Bess put him to bed, fed him broth, kept the children outside as well as she could, and over time, although he did not regain his lost weight, his strength returned.

He told her all that had happened since he had left. She told him that with eight young ones she'd been about ready to give up the ghost; they needed their father, but mostly, she told him, they needed discipline, particularly the boys.

It was a good time. These homecomings usually were. As Davy gained weight, he would take one of two of the boys hunting.

The land was not as full of game as it had been. Settlers were clearing land, building cabins, even coming together on Sundays for hours of prayer and worship.

They had either killed off the surplus game or had driven it out of the area. Davy, who had for years never returned without meat, bear or deer or turkey, had to go farther even to find sign of game.

He told Bess about the country he had seen, about the abundance of game, clearings with rich grass, and probably because she recognized the signs, she became resigned to another move.

This time to a territory she genuinely liked. It was on the South Fork of the Obion River in the Tennessee wilderness.

There were other settlers but miles distant. The ground would grow anything planted in it. There were open places that required no clearing, and that eight half-wild youngsters could explore in all directions. It was virgin country that abounded with game.

Davy was pleased that Bess liked the area and set about cutting logs for a house, a larger one this time, with a wide loft for the children.

He was happy, busy, in good health, and under his wife's solicitous care put on weight. She got him a new buckskin hunting shirt and trousers, even new moccasins. He visited a few settlements, returned with powder and lead, cloth for Bess to make dresses for the girls, and small presents. What money he had came from his wife. Rarely in his life did Davy Crockett have money for even small purchases.

He was a dead shot. When the opportunity arose, he went to shooting matches, and while he invariably won prizes, they usually were shoats, turkeys, a half side of beef, or jugs of whiskey. Money in Crockett's part of the nation was scarce. When it was offered, it usually was Spanish silver pieces of eight. The United States did not begin to mint its own money in any quantities for many years, so the silver of frontier America remained the Spanish piece of eight.

People bartered, took goods and livestock in exchange for labor. Davy Crockett was only one of hundreds of people living on the frontier who never had much money. For most items essential for survival they did not need it. There was no paper currency, and, when it was eventually issued, it was scorned, called "shin plasters," and commerce and trade ignored it in favor of coinage.

CHAPTER
FIVE

Gone Hunting

The Obion River country provided everything a family required to survive. Davy's passion was hunting. He kept the family supplied with a variety of meat ranging from green turtles to wild fowl and bear.

Not everyone on the frontier was partial to bear meat. Bess Crockett devised ways of cooking it that made it palatable. Davy killed dozens of bears. Meat his family did not need he gave to others. His reputation as a hunter spread. He often took one of the boys with him, usually John Wesley. In time John Wesley also became a renowned hunter.

Bess's brother moved into the area. His place was six miles from the Crockett property, which was close enough.

Davy's bear-hunting not only provided meat and hides, it also provided danger. Hunting with dogs in late spring with humidity high and the weather beginning to turn warm, he followed the sounding of his dogs into a clearing and came face to face with a huge black bear that was at bay, but, since the dogs would not attack, the bear had room to maneuver and climbed a tree. Crockett shot him. It required two bullets to bring the bear to the ground.

Davy's dogs went after the wounded bear that acted as though no bullets had struck him. Davy could not fire again for fear of hitting the dogs. With hounds around him, darting in to bite and jump clear, the bear roared and was too occupied with dogs to heed the man with the rifle.

Davy waited until the huge animal was lying on its side before approaching with his drawn knife. Without warning the bear got to its feet and lunged, making a savage swipe with one paw. It then reared up to its full height and charged. Davy had left his rifle leaning against a tree. He tried to jump clear, barely eluded the massive paws, and slashed as the bear went past.

The huge animal came around, snarling, slobbering, and was poised for another charge. Davy back-pedaled toward the tree where his rifle was leaning. The bear came after him on all fours, moving deliberately, snarling as it came. Davy's problem was that after his second shot he had leaned the rifle aside without reloading it.

He got the rifle and continued to retreat. The bear did not charge again. It came after the man with a ponderous snarling stride that neither increased nor slackened.

Davy used trees, deadfalls, every distraction at hand to avoid the bear while he reloaded. When he was ready, he took a stand, watched the bear coming straight at him, and shot it the third time. This time the ball pierced the heart.

He was more than ten miles from home with night approaching. If he left the bear until the following day, wolves and other varmints would get it.

He went home, got his brother-in-law to return with him, and, following blazes he'd made with his tomahawk, led four pack animals through the night to the site of the dead bear.

By firelight they butchered the bear, loaded the animals with meat and the hide, and struck out for home. It was a cold, dark night, and they did not reach the Crockett clearing until about dawn.

The hide of the huge bear as well as other hides Davy had cured made quite a load. He took them to a town named Alexander and sold them.

With the credit he purchased supplies — flour, sugar, coffee, salt, lead slugs to make musket balls, powder, some toys for the children — and returned home.

As time passed, Crockett's seclusion was interrupted several times by tales of atrocities perpetrated by roving bands of renegades. Some bands were mixed Indians and whites. There was no law. Guns, knives, and tomahawks preserved what peace there was, but because raids by renegade bands were unpredictable, even men working the land did so with weapons at hand.

Davy was hunting several miles from home when he caught the scent of a cooking fire. He was deep in forested country where there were no settlers for miles and no roads, only game trails.

He moved cautiously toward the scent of cooking where smoke arose in a small clearing. From within the forest's fringe he saw six men in buckskin around the fire. They were eating meat from a deer they had killed. He did not recognize any of them.

They had hobbled horses grazing the clearing. They also had something else — two bedraggled women whose faces showed purple swellings. The younger of the women had a bloody bandage on her lower left arm.

Davy hid in underbrush. He was satisfied he could kill one, perhaps two of the renegades before they located him by gunpowder smoke, but that left four.

He watched the horses. There was no way to reach them, turn them loose, and set the renegades afoot. He had a ruse that was commonly used on the frontier — the scream of a mountain lion called a panther — but while that might draw off several of the renegades, it would not make all of them leave the camp and the women.

He was too far from the cabin of his brother-in-law or other settlers to go back and return. Renegades did not linger; they ate, slept, and continually moved.

What he needed was a distraction of sufficient interest to make all the renegades leave the camp. If there was such a diversion, he could not think of it.

One of the renegades left the fire, walked in Davy's direction, then veered to the right, and disappeared in a spit of trees that projected a few yards into the clearing.

He was a bearded bear of a man who walked with a slight limp. Davy, who feared nothing that walked, crawled, or climbed, left his place of concealment heading in a roundabout way for the spit of trees. He moved very carefully.

He was close to the trees where the large bearded man had disappeared when the man left the forest, walking back toward the camp. He was carrying a jug. When the others saw what he had, they called out in profane anticipation. The bearded man reached the camp and laughed as he wrenched the corncob from the mouth of the jug.

One renegade across the fire called out: "Henry, you had it hid, damn you!"

The bearded man replied gruffly. "It warn't hid. I just left it in them trees till we'd et."

A red-headed man said: "Where'd you get it? I didn't see you carryin' it."

"I found it in the wood shed of that settler we burned out yestiddy." The bearded man held the jug aloft. "He won't have no need for it . . . not where he's goin'."

Davy found the place where the bearded man had put the jug. He found something else, a broken necklace with a cameo in its center. He picked it up, scoured close around for whatever might be in sight, and found a pistol with a broken handle. It had been used to club someone; there was dried blood and some hair embedded in the shattered wood. But the other thing he found was significant — in a roll of filthy blankets was a pouch of shag tobacco that also held a clay pipe. This was where the big bearded man had left his gatherings. This was where he would bed down.

Davy returned to the forest's fringe, listened to the men get louder as the jug was passed around, and decided finally what he would do.

It was a long wait. The renegades piled wood onto the fire, spoke loudly, became more boisterous and careless even after the jug had been flung aside, empty.

Dusk arrived. They kept the fire burning high enough to throw light in all directions and Davy watched, listened, and waited. Not until the men drifted away one by one to their bed ground did he move closer to the place where the bearded man would sleep.

The red-headed man and the renegade with the limp sat hunkered at the fire after the others had departed. Davy could not hear what they said, but he could guess from the way the women clung close to each other, their faces made phantom-like by firelight.

The red-headed man got angry and raised his voice. "I tol' you, Henry, I take the young one, an' no damned argument!"

There was no argument. The bearded man simply arose, looked across the fire, and jerked his head for the older woman to follow. She clutched the younger woman and whimpered. The red-headed man laughed derisively. "She allows you're too ugly, Henry."

The big bearded man started around the fire. The women held one another and cringed. Henry grabbed the older woman by the hair. When the younger woman would not release her, Henry stepped close and swung a massive fist. The younger woman collapsed. Henry then half dragged, half kicked, and punched the older woman toward the spit of trees.

Behind him the red-headed man walked around the fire, stood looking at the unconscious younger woman who had blood running from a torn mouth, and called after the bearded man: "You ruint this one. I'll take the old one."

Henry turned with a snarl. "That's the one you wanted, that's the one you get." He then dragged and punched the older woman to his bed ground.

Davy did not move until the bearded man reached his spit of trees. He did as he'd done in the bear fight. He left his rifle leaning against a tree, soundlessly made a wide half circle until he was behind the bearded man, who was roughly yanking his blankets flat on the ground. The bearded man looked at the older woman and said: "What'd you say your name was?"

"Rebecca Holt."

"Rebecca, you seen what happened to your friend. You do as I say or you'll get the same only worse."

The woman had both legs raised and encircled with her arms. She said: "What do you want? My husband's got some horses. We got some gold money hid."

Henry stood over the woman, expressionless and massive. "If we'd wanted them horses, we'd have took them. Gold? You're lyin' for a fact. Now get your clothes off an' get into them blankets, an', if you get to cryin', I'll cut your ears off, an' your husband won't want you after that. Shed them clothes!"

The woman whimpered as she began unbuttoning her dress. Davy did not make a sound as he crept closer. He kept the man's back to him so that, if the woman saw movement, she would not gasp or speak.

Henry was not a patient man. He leaned, caught hold of cloth, and wrenched so hard the woman was twisted onto one side. She opened her mouth to scream. Henry didn't hit her. He simply caught her by the hair and clamped a huge hand over her mouth.

Davy was close when the bearded man removed his hand, slapped the woman so hard her head snapped sideways.

Davy took ten long steps and plunged the knife deep. The big man tried to turn, his face contorted. Davy hit him as hard as he could. The big man fell backward atop the woman. She pushed clear. There was blood on her dress, arms, and hands. She sat staring at it.

Davy rolled the man over, withdrew the knife, got the woman on her feet, and led her away. She moved mechanically as silent as stone. When he got back where the rifle leaned, he pushed her gently to the ground. She looked straight at him from eyes that did not seem to focus. He spoke to her in a low voice.

"Stay quiet. Set here an' don't make no noise."

When she spoke, her voice was little more than a whisper. "I don't know . . . I didn't see you. Are you one of 'em?"

"No ma'am, my name's Crockett. I was huntin' an' smelt their cooking fire. Stay quiet. You're well hid." Davy did not want to leave the woman. He feared she might come out of her deep shock and cry out.

He reached to touch her hand. She cringed and yanked the hand away. Davy leaned back, looking at her. He was still looking at her when she spoke. "Crockett? Are you Davy Crockett? My husband shot against you one time for a brace of turkeys. He said you was the best shooter he ever seen."

Davy relaxed slightly. "Did you hear what I said?"

"About bein' quiet an' not movin'?"

"Yes."

"An' you'll come back . . . because I don't know where I am."

"I'll come back. You just get hold of yourself and be still."

He took the rifle and watched for movement. There was none. The fire was down to red coals. He was straining for sound when he heard a whimper from across the clearing. He started around in that direction, using the trees to shield him from detection. Because the under turf was thick and spongy he made no sound.

It was a long hike and a slow one. There were other renegades bedded down. In the clearing the horses followed his progress with heads raised, little ears pointing. Man scent was easy to detect on a still night.

Across the clearing he had no difficulty locating the area where the whimpering sound had come from. A man was cursing. Davy heard him strike yielding flesh and tracked that sound to a little creek with soft earth and grass along its bank.

There were creek willows on both sides of the watercourse. Beyond them the forest was thick and dark.

He stepped behind a large tree to listen. Although his eyes were accustomed to darkness, he could not make out any detail for more than about twenty feet, but movement was visible in an area where nothing moved. The red-headed man was sitting back on his heels. On the ground before him was the younger woman. When she cried, he hit her.

Davy crept around the place where the man was kneeling. He stopped when the man said: "I'm goin' to kill you for kickin' me, you bitch."

A twig broke under Davy's foot.

The red-headed man whirled, then sprang upright. He started to sidle toward a log where his powder horn, shot pouch, and rifle had been put aside.

Davy moved in the same direction, keeping near trees and not making a sound. The red-headed man reached the log first. He reached for a belt. Davy saw the pistol in his fist as the renegade straightened up. Davy waited until the man was peering in the direction where the twig had snapped before raising his rifle. The red-headed man caught movement from the side and whirled as he crouched. Davy had to aim again. The red-headed man fired his handgun. The sound shattered the silence. The ball struck a tree three feet to the left of Crockett.

The renegade dropped behind the log. Davy could not see him. He watched for the renegade to reach for his rifle. When that happened, Davy fired. The old punky log splintered, the leaning rifle fell on Davy's side of the log, and both powder horn and shot pouch fell on the renegade's side of the log. He would at least be able to reload the pistol.

Davy gave him no time for that. He came across the old log in one bound. The red-headed man struggled to get to his feet. Davy slashed with the knife, heard the renegade suck air as he sprang aside, then Davy went straight at the man.

Of one thing he was certain. Gunshots in the night would awaken the other renegades. Whether they would seek the cause or be prudent and wary, he did not know. What he *did* know was that the red-headed man was strong, quick, and wiry.

Davy moved carefully, stalking him. He tried to maneuver the renegade so that his back would be to the log, but the red-headed man was too experienced to let that happen.

He did allow himself to be driven to the log where he grabbed his rifle. Davy sprang at the man. There was no time to use the rifle so the red-headed man swung it like a club.

Davy got under the gun, came up inside it, and lunged as the red-headed man was trying hard to recover from the sideways momentum of his wild swing. Davy was in front of him with the knife rising. The renegade made a sound deep in his throat, dropped the rifle, and went backward over the log. Only his feet showed. Davy's big knife was half buried in the renegade's chest.

Davy went to the woman, who had wrapped herself in a blanket, got her to her feet, told her she had to move fast, and led off back the way he had come.

When he reached the older woman, she stood up and locked her arms around the younger woman. They cried.

Davy took his rifle with him, went out where the horses were, left the hobbles lying in the grass, and fired his rifle to stampede the animals.

They fled southward into the forest. He could still hear them when he got back to the women, told them there was no time to lose, and led off in a half trot that they did not have the strength to emulate so he had to let them rest several times before he got back in familiar territory.

If they were being pursued, Davy neither heard nor saw any sign of it. It was unlikely; nothing was more important to renegades than mounts. Even if the surviving men found their two dead companions, it would not mean as much as finding their horses.

The last time the women rested there was a creek where they could wash blood off and do what they could to make themselves presentable, which was not very much.

It was the younger woman who began to lag and wander, to cringe when Davy came close. He told the older woman to stay with her friend while he scouted.

The only thing he saw when dawn arrived was smoke rising from the chimney of his cabin. He went back, found the women sitting on the ground, got them to their feet, and from here on he set his pace to theirs. The need for haste was past.

When he entered the clearing, some of the children saw him and ran to tell Bess. She came out front, wiping both hands on her apron as she watched the bone-tired women following her husband.

She had once told John Wesley, who was standing nearby, that when his father went hunting only God knew what he would return with.

CHAPTER
SIX

A Small Boy on a Big Horse

The women had been stolen from a small settlement forty miles southwest. Davy sent word where the women were and that they were safe.

Six days later five armed men arrived out front of the cabin. Two of them were the husbands of the stolen women.

The reunion was tearful. The settlers wanted to know where Davy had found the women. They also wanted to know about the renegades. Davy told them he would guide them back to the clearing, but whether the surviving renegades had recovered their horses or not, too much time had passed. Even renegades on foot would no longer be in the country.

He had been home eight days when a gaunt, taciturn man riding a horse with two feathers braided into its mane behind one ear rode up, climbed down, tied his animal, and met Bess in the doorway. She had recently fed the chickens and was about ready to start a meal.

When she met the older man in buckskin and saw the feathers on the horse, she had a foreboding, but because Davy was out with John Wesley, checking their traps, she invited the older man inside. When Davy did not return in time for supper, she fed him, and, when the children asked questions, the stranger gave minimal answers.

He ate until Bess thought he must have worms. He also drank three cups of coffee. With dusk approaching, he went out front, fired up a little pipe, and sat on a bench, watching his horse eat.

Bess told the children not to bother the man, and in fact because of his preoccupied and taciturn manner the children peered around the corner of the house at him but otherwise kept their distance.

Davy and John Wesley returned with two big tom turkeys they had shot and a string of traps from which the animals had been removed and skinned.

As Davy came across the clearing, the stranger knocked dottle from his pipe and arose from the bench. Before entering the house, he had leaned his rifle against the wall outside. He waited until Davy was close, then said: "Howdy. Is that your boy?"

Davy handed the rifles to John Wesley, dropped the hides and traps, and greeted the older man. "He's that. Jesse, you're a distance from home."

"Got no home," Jesse Jones said. "Maraudin' Choctaws burnt me out."

"Have you et?"

"Your woman cooks up a fine meal. I liked to eat you out of house and grits. Davy, they're runnin' wild. Burnt out some cabins, killed folks, run off livestock, and fought a pitched battle at a settlement."

Davy sat on a bench. "Choctaws?"

"Yes. From somewhere in that easterly strip. I think the Army went to make 'em move, an' they took up the hatchet. They even raided some Creek an' Cherokee settlements. They was like wild men, painted an' armed with British guns left over from Jackson's war." Jesse Jones sat down, gazing out where it was barely possible to discern his horse. "I warn't home. Was out huntin'. Just as well, I expect. I heard the noise, seen the smoke startin', and hurried back. Looked like maybe twenty, thirty. They'd taken my Army horse and was leavin' when I come out of the trees. One hung back to kill some chickens. I crept up an' busted his head. That's his horse out yonder."

Davy asked where the soldiers were. They were supposed to be policing the land acquired from Indians. Jesse Jones simply shook his head. He was too demoralized to make one of the common remarks about the Army. He said: "They'll head this way, which is why I come. Davy, there's too many. For all I know it ain't just that one band. You got neighbors?"

"Some. Not close," Davy said, and stood up. "We'll fix you a place inside."

Jesse also arose. "You got room? I can bed down outside. How many kids you got?"

"Eight. Fetch your blankets. You can sleep by the fireplace."

"I don't expect your wife'll cotton to a stranger traipsin' in. I can bed down outside."

Davy said: "Where's your saddle?"

They went where Jesse had left his outfit. Davy untied the blankets, tossed them over one shoulder, and said: "Why'd you say they'd be headin' this way?"

"Because they burnt out and raided from east to west. That don't have to mean they'll come this far, but it don't pay not to look out a little."

With the tolerance only a woman with eight children could possess, Bess Crockett made Jesse Jones comfortable, even brought him a cup of broth as he and her husband sat, watching the fire. After she had used her apron like a woman herding chickens to get the children to bed, Jesse said: "I never married. I never run across a woman like yours. I never stopped lookin, but it's gettin' kind of late now."

He put the emptied cup aside and watched flames leap for a moment before also saying: "I'm half a mind to go north where they got more people, big towns, and got the redskins tamed. That was the fourth cabin I've built. Can't even get in a decent stand of corn nor potatoes ready before someone rides across the crops or shoots my chickens."

Davy got a jug of corn squeezings, but Jesse Jones's mood was too deep to be affected by whiskey, although he drank right along with his host.

When he arose before bedding down, he said: "Somethin's got to be done, Davy, or we might just as well give it all back to the Indians. Good night."

Davy told Bess what Jones had said. While she lay abed at his side, the foreboding returned. But she had never argued with Davy. She did not say much this time except that the hostiles might not come this far.

In the morning, when Davy's brood was gathered for breakfast, Jesse Jones was not in the house. Davy went to find him. Jesse was sitting on the ground near his

Indian horse, smoking his pipe. He exchanged greetings with Davy, removed the pipe, and said: "I'll move on. You got about all the cabin will hold."

Davy squatted. "Move on . . . where?"

"Just move on. I don't want to build another cabin an' have it burnt down. Up north maybe."

Davy considered his buckskin-clad friend with the fox-skin hat and shook his head. "You'd come back. Too many folks, no good hunting, too many farms cut up the land."

Jones relit his pipe.

When her man entered the house with the older man trailing, Bess heaped two plates with venison, biscuits, and the sweet from a bee tree, filled cups with chicory-flavored coffee, and herded the children outside.

She built up the fire, told Jesse she'd made a bed for him in the shed off the back of the cabin, and told him he could stay as long as he cared to. Jesse watched her feed the fire, clear away plates to be washed, looked at Davy, and said: "You done right proud with that 'un, Davy."

Jesse helped Davy with the chores after which they sat on the porch to talk. Davy had thought long and hard about what Jesse had told him.

It hadn't ended with Red Eagle's defeat at Horseshoe Bend. Maybe it would never end, but he doubted that because, like it or not, the territory was filling up. Eventually the Indians would be overwhelmed. In the meantime he had no intention of waiting for raiders to reach as far as his homestead.

He told Jesse he had two neighbors, Luke Biggs and Tom Fite. He would visit them, repeat what Jesse had told him, and see if they would go over the countryside spreading the alarm.

When Jesse asked how many men might be recruited, Davy had to guess. "Twenty, maybe a tad more."

Jesse was unimpressed. "It won't be enough. There was more'n that in the band that burnt me out, an' my guess is there's other bands. Maybe they got Creeks an' Cherokees with 'em. No soldiers around?"

None that Davy knew of. The forts were scattered. Soldiers patrolled occasionally but not often and never stayed long. He said he figured they'd ought to depend on themselves and whatever help they could scare up.

Jesse went with him. As they were crossing out of the clearing, Bess watched from the doorway. Every time Davy left, she had misgivings about his ever returning. Later generations would call it the law of averages. With Bess Crockett it was something closer to the heart.

Davy and Jesse were gone four days. The homesteads in the Obion River country were widely scattered. No one had neighbors closer than several miles. As far as the menfolk were concerned, this was close enough. How the womenfolk felt about isolation was moot.

They got Luke Biggs to ride the countryside with the alarm. Tom Fite probably would have agreed to do the same, but, when they reached his clearing, Tom was flat on his back, drenched with sweat, shivering like he was freezing. His woman said it was one of those attacks that came onto her man from time to time.

70

On the fifth day they returned to Davy's clearing, hadn't been there long enough to off-saddle and turn the horses out, when a youngster not much older than John Wesley came into the yard on a twelve-hundred-pound, pudding-footed, big harness horse that had been ridden too hard. As the youth slid to the ground, words tumbled out of him. He was tow-headed, thin, big-eyed, and clearly near the end of his tether.

He said his name was Reno Knight. His father was James Knight who farmed some distance south of the Obion settlement. All but the big horse he had been riding had been run off in the night. His father's hired man, who had gone out to do chores at daybreak, had been killed by an arrow, not sixty feet from the house.

The lad knew little more. His father had told him how to reach the pudding-footed horse behind the cabin, had told him to ride for help. He had given the alarm in the settlement and had been told to keep riding until he found the Crockett homestead. They had told him at the settlement Davy Crockett knew more about fighting Indians than anyone around.

The lad was shaking although the morning was warm. Jesse took him to the house, handed him over to Bess. The Crockett children were still and silent for once as Bess led the lad to stand by the fire until she got him a cup of hot broth.

Davy was waiting with the horses when Jesse returned. Before mounting, Davy handed Jesse the rifle he called Betsy, got astride, and led off southward. This time neither his wife nor the children saw him leave, but come chore time with both saddle animals gone it required no figuring to know that the horses had not gone off by themselves.

Bess and the children listened to the frightened boy from south of the settlement, and, while the children were fascinated by the youthful stranger, Bess refused to allow her mind to dwell on the absence of her man.

Because of the humidity, Davy and Jesse did not push their horses. It was Jesse's opinion that pushing the animals to their limit was not going to have much to do with what had probably already happened, and he was right.

Men from the settlement had gone south, but, when they heard no gunfire, decided that continuing toward the Knight clearing would very likely let them ride into an ambush, and turned back.

When Davy and Jesse reached the settlement, it was quiet. People nodded to the pair of strangers in buckskin but did not approach them.

Two stores had steel shutters closed with locked doors behind them. They went to the tavern that had, besides the proprietor, two customers, both freighters whose outfits were on the edge of town.

The barman set up two ales, accepted Davy's money, and walked away. One of the freighters, a graying, bearded man with a scar on his forehead said his name was Birch Newton. He also said he recognized Davy from seeing him at several shooting matches.

Davy introduced Jesse and asked the freighter where the Knight clearing was. The other freighter, short and bear-built, spoke without looking around. "About two miles south on the east side of the trace. You know 'em, do you?"

Davy explained about the lad on the big work horse. The short man still did not face Crockett. He considered his half empty cup of ale and said: "No point in goin' there, mister. There's nothin' left. We seen the smoke an' the fire last night." The freighter finally faced Davy. "There won't be nothin' left. If the lad got away, he'll be the only one who did."

The tavernkeeper added more. "The Knights ain't the only ones. We seen other fires last night. Red Sticks, mister, we could hear 'em howlin'."

Davy and Jesse left the settlement. They also left the trace, rode where the land was heavily forested, stopped often to listen. Jesse said: "Long gone. You heard what the tavernkeeper said."

Jesse was right. When they came to the clearing they thought had to have belonged to James Knight, they left the horses hidden and moved carefully to the fringe of the clearing.

They saw a sow that had been shot, a milk cow with so many arrows in her she looked like a pincushion — and a woman face down with one arm outstretched to touch the hand of a burly, tow-headed man who had four arrows in him, any one of which would have caused death.

Several chickens lay where arrows had pierced them. Jesse leaned on his rifle and softly swore. When he finished, he said: "Least we can do is bury 'em."

That was what they did, using spades and crowbars they found in an unburned shed. They did not talk.

After the wooden crosses had been pounded into the ground, Davy removed his coon-skin hat and said a simple prayer.

Jesse did not speak until they were back with the horses. "Why'd you pray over 'em?" he asked.

Davy's answer was cryptic. "Because I'm a Christian and because it's decent to pray over dead folks."

Jesse was swinging into the saddle when he said: "They don't need no send-off, Davy. They needed prayers to be answered while they was alive."

Davy sat, cradling Betsy and considering the westerly forest. "Jesse, seems to me them folks in that settlement got no grit in their craws." He jutted his jaw Indian fashion. "There's the trail."

Instead of speaking, the older man nudged his horse out into the upper end of the clearing and angled southward until he came to the sign of many riders. He paused to cheek a cud of molasses-cured tobacco, offered the twist to Davy, and said: "I ain't sure just the two of us can do much, but settin' down an' waitin' for them folks from your country to get together and head down this way just might let a lot of settlers get caught like these folks was."

They cut the trail and had little difficulty staying on it. Aside from trampled ground they found scraps of women's clothing, some pots and pans, an axe with a shattered handle, and a large shaving mug with the initials JK on it.

The raiders were passing through some dense, dark forest. Davy studied the sign and told Jesse he did not believe the Indians knew the country. He knew it, and anyone else who did would have gone north where there was more open country and, incidentally, where there were more isolated homesteads.

The day was ending. Dusk was coming. Davy was watching for a creek where they could make camp, when a loud howl broke the forest's hush.

Jesse nodded and dismounted. "They're close. I got no idea why they ain't miles from here, but that was a Red Stick yell if I ever heard one."

They left the horses tethered in a concealing thicket and went warily and silently in the direction of that yell.

They heard deep growling noises as the trees thinned out and eventually did not grow at all except for five or six trees in a grassy clearing.

Davy caught Jesse's arm. A large black bear with an arrow in his rump had an Indian on the ground. How he had managed to accomplish this was anyone's guess, but the Indian was dead. Blood was everywhere in the grass and underbrush. The bear was not satisfied. He continued to bite, growl, and fling the body from side to side.

There was no sign of the Indian's horse, but there wouldn't be, not after the horse caught bear scent. Jesse made a conjecture. "He was tryin' to catch the others. His horse smelt bear an' run out from under him. He got off one arrer, then the bear done the rest."

It was as good a guess as any other. They returned for the horses and made a big wide sashay around the area where the bear was still growling and worrying the dead Indian.

The trail veered slightly northward. That many mounted men could not avoid leaving abundant sign. Davy and Jesse followed it like a pair of hounds right up until it became difficult to see tracks. Between day's end and forest gloom they had to dismount and track on foot, which was a slow, exasperating method. If it had any advantage, it might be that the raiders would make camp, and, if they did, and if Davy and Jesse continued to track them, they would close the distance.

They had to stop when no moon appeared. It would not have helped much anyway in forested country where treetops prevented both sunlight and moonlight from reaching the ground except in rare places.

Where they halted, trees were not entirely dense. There were clumps of buffalo grass, about the only thing that would grow, and some wild pigeons arrived to perch for the night.

Davy watched them arrive and shook his head. A gunshot would be heard a long way. He and Jesse would eat tomorrow if they were lucky.

They took turns sleeping. Davy was convinced the raiders were no more than a mile or two ahead.

CHAPTER
SEVEN

Caught!

They were in the saddle ahead of sunrise. There was a faint scent of wood smoke that they tracked with caution. Renegades, white or red, were as wary as wolves. When the scent was strong, they left the horses, crept ahead, found a nest of downed timber in the middle of which was a huge wood-rat nest.

Here, Davy held up his hand. They stopped. The wood rat, the size of a house cat, came out, wrinkled his nose, swapped ends, and disappeared back inside his house.

The smoke scent became stronger. Jesse went out a few yards, sniffed like a bear, and returned to say: "They'd ought to be a-horseback by now."

Davy made a guess. "That settler back yonder more'n likely had a jug."

A flock of frightened birds passed overhead. The men exchanged a look. Davy led off in a northwesterly direction. The smoke scent became stronger, and the next time they halted it was because a man up ahead somewhere called to someone in a language Jesse Jones understood. He leaned to whisper. "They're arguin' about goin' ahead or goin' back an' attackin' the settlement."

They listened to the arguing Indians until a man with a deep, loud voice told the arguers to be quiet. They would go northwest. They could raid the settlement on their way back.

Davy lifted Betsy to cradle her in his arm, and Jesse was jettisoning the cud of molasses-cured that he had substituted for breakfast, when an arrow struck chest high on a half-grown redbud between them.

Davy dropped flat. Jesse hesitated just long enough to peer in the direction from which the arrow had come, and the second arrow came from a different direction. It struck the barrel of Jesse's rifle. The impact half spun Jones who also dropped.

Moments passed. There was not a sound. They were exposed to the south and to the west, but that first arrow had come from the east. The second one had come from the west. Davy squirmed until he was facing easterly.

Nothing happened. Davy swore under his breath. "They're cuttin' around us."

Jesse grunted.

Someone with a deep voice called to them. "You, stand up!"

Davy called back: "Not likely."

This time the arrow struck the ground between them. It was followed by the same deep, rough voice that now ordered them for the second time to stand up.

They arose, holding their rifles held low, cocked and ready.

The invisible Indian told them to put their weapons on the ground.

Davy put Betsy on the ground and straightened up as Jesse leaned to do the same. Each of them still had a fleshing knife and a hatchet.

A stocky, dark Indian moved into view from behind a tree. He was holding a flintlock pistol. Something about him was familiar to Davy. The Indian walked closer, aimed his pistol at Davy's soft parts, and spoke: "You know me?"

Davy shook his head. "I've seen you somewhere, can't rightly recollect where it was."

"At the village where you kept soldiers from attacking. You told that bushy-headed captain to go away. We run off their horses."

Davy's gaze widened. He remembered. He did not know the Indian's name but he remembered him as the sullen, dark man.

Jesse spoke: "You're Charley Ben. We stampeded them Army horses."

The dark Indian nodded in Jesse's direction. "You Jesse."

For five seconds, with more Indians arriving on all sides of the white men, nothing more was said. But eventually the man called Charley Ben spoke again, but in his own language, and four Indians came up behind the white men, roughly grabbed them, swung them around, and punched them in the direction of their camp.

The raiders watched them arrive. Every one of them had a rifle, most had hatchets, and all had big knives in sheaths with the fur side out.

Their breakfast fire was down to coals and no longer gave off much smoke. The captives were pushed to the ground. There were bridled horses. There were also bags of loot. The Indians had been ready to mount up and depart.

The buck who had shot the first arrow, a pale-skinned half-breed with black eyes and hair took the rifles and said something that Jesse understood but did not interpret. Davy had heard the term many times. Most Indian languages lacked profanity, but they had no trouble learning from whites. They usually embellished curses with a few words of their own. Among other things he had called them scalp locks.

The Indians were restless. They were aware of the peril of remaining in one place very long.

Charley Ben retained his sullen expression when he squatted in front of the captives. "Time you die," he said.

Davy's answer should have appealed to Charley Ben because of what he and Jesse had done — saved an entire village from being massacred by soldiers. With other Indians it probably would have been grounds for release, but these were renegades, haters of whites, men who wanted only to kill, destroy, plunder, and burn.

Charley Ben's expression showed no hint of gratitude. When Davy reminded him of the village, Charley Ben said: "Yesterday. Many yesterdays. We take scalps from soldiers, too. From all people who don't belong in our country."

That large half-breed Indian who had been with the spokesman in the village Davy had saved pushed through his companions and spoke to Charley Ben. He spit out words of contempt. "Big warrior. Davy Crockett big hunter, bear fighter. Big warrior." The large half-breed took the hatchet from his belt. "I am Many Scalps."

Charley Ben looked from the rangy, tall white man to the pale-skinned, muscular large warrior and said: "Do it fast. We got to leave here."

Jesse glanced at the Indian who had their rifles. He also had their hatchets and knives. The Indian looked back and made a mirthless smile.

Davy did not move. There was a long moment when no one made a sound. Many Scalps moved on the balls of his feet, like a stalking mountain lion. He did not raise his tomahawk. His black eyes never left Davy's face. Davy remembered this buck, but only that he was large and powerfully built. Now he understood something else. Many Scalps had probably earned his name as an experienced fighter.

He half circled Crockett, his intention to make Davy move his feet, a man with one foot in the air could not move as swiftly as a man balancing forward on the balls of his feet.

There was not a sound. The renegades anticipated a swift killing. When Davy had to shift position, he did not raise a foot. He scuffed dust as he kept both feet on the ground.

Many Scalps hesitated, stepped back, let the hatchet hang briefly at his side, then, with an unnerving scream, he raised the hand axe and charged.

Davy waited until the axe arm was rising, when Many Scalps was less than two feet in his headlong charge, whipped sideways, and gave ground. As the big half-breed brought his axe down where Davy had been, Crockett hit him under the ear with a rock-hard fist. The blow would have put most men flat down. It dazed Many Scalps, who staggered and gave ground until his eyes focused. He wasn't hurt and began to sidle sideways, almost past Davy and out of arm's reach, then swung around, and again raised the axe.

This time, as Davy moved, the Indian holding Betsy and Jesse's rifle shoved a gun butt out. As Davy fell and rolled to get one hand braced to arise, Jesse swore at the Indian who had tripped Crockett. Otherwise there was not a sound.

Many Scalps hurled himself at Crockett before Davy could stand up. He rolled frantically but Many Scalps still struck him as he fell. His axe missed Davy's head by at least twelve inches. It buried itself in the ground close to the foot of the renegade with the captured rifles who jumped furiously and someone laughed.

Davy got onto all fours as Many Scalps struggled to reach a position where he could use the hatchet. Davy kicked, watched the hatchet sail in the direction of the spectators, then got upright. When Many Scalps was coming up off the ground, he hit him again, this time rolling his shoulder in behind the blow. In the deathly hush it sounded like someone bursting a gourd.

Many Scalps fell into the arms of two onlookers who roughly pushed him around and shoved him ahead.

This time Davy moved out of the way as Many Scalps grabbed for air and went down on all fours, and hung there like a gut-shot bear. For moments the Indians stared at Davy, who, as victor, had the right of killing Many Scalps.

Jesse held out Davy's coon-skin hat, which Crockett put on and turned to go over beside the dazed Indian on all fours. He hoisted him upright, jutted his jaw in the direction of the half-buried tomahawk, and said: "Get it."

The big half-breed had one eye closing. There was a thin, flung-back streamer of blood at the corner of his mouth. He met Davy's eyes from a distance of no more than fifteen inches until the Indian with the captured rifles leaned them aside, retrieved the tomahawk, pushed ahead, and put it into the hand of the big half-breed.

Davy roughly shoved Many Scalps away. Charley Ben growled at the big half-breed: "You make hurry, dammit!"

Many Scalps had been hurt, but something else had happened to him. For the first time in his life he knew fear. Several raiders snarled at him. He shook his head like a bear in bee time and shuffled forward. Davy waited.

Jesse wrenched the hatchet from the belt of a warrior standing with him, walked over, and handed it to Davy. He then walked back, looking straight into the face of the man from whom he'd taken the hatchet. That Indian said nothing. None of them did.

This time it was Davy who began the stalk. This time it was the muscular half-breed who shuffled dust so he would always be able to face Crockett as he retreated.

An Indian called to Many Scalps: "You quit! I finish." His tone had been contemptuous. All the bystanders understood. Another Indian called to Many Scalps, and this time the words stung: "No Many Scalps. Many Skirts!"

Indians laughed. Charley Ben stood up, dusted off, and said: "We go. Get horses. Too much time gone here." He looked among his followers, selected an older man, and said: "You kill white men. We go. You catch up."

The older buck was the Indian who had the captured rifles. He did not watch his companions move off in the direction of patiently standing horses. He looked from Many Scalps to Crockett who was stalking his adversary, this time with equal armament. He could not shoot as long as Davy was between him and Many Scalps so he moved a little to one side.

Jesse called to him to effect a diversion. As the renegade half swung to face Jesse, Davy sprang. This time Many Scalps not only did not raise his hatchet, he back-pedaled.

Davy's momentum carried him ahead so fast they collided. Only then did Many Scalps raise his axe. It was too late. Davy struck him hard on the side of the head with the flat side of his tomahawk.

The result was that this time when Many Scalps went down he stayed down. As Davy bent over, the old Indian hastily fired. The musket ball struck a tree chest-high where Davy had been standing before leaning down.

Jesse picked up Many Scalps's axe and hurled it as hard as he could. It did not strike the older Indian but it came close enough to make him flinch.

Jesse ran at the renegade who had no time to reload before Jesse reached him. The blow was overhand and descended as hard as Jesse could make it. The Indian was dead before he hit the ground.

Jesse reached for his rifle, fired it into the air, and then, with both rifles, joined Davy in the race to the place where they had left their horses.

As they got astride, Jesse tried to reload. He spilled more powder than he was able to get into the muzzle. They did not make haste, but they remained on the trail. Where they stopped before crossing a burned-over clearing, Davy asked about that second shot. Jesse answered in the matter-of-fact way that was typical of him.

"He was supposed to kill two of us. That second shot would carry a considerable distance. I figured if they didn't hear two shots, maybe one of 'em might have come back."

They were heading in the general direction of the Crockett homestead, slightly more westerly, but the farther upcountry the renegades rode, the greater was the possibility that they would find isolated farms — and settlers.

They were remaining in the trees as much as they could, but by late afternoon the trail they were following began to veer more to the west.

Davy knew they would have scouts out. He also knew the country into which the renegades were heading and it had quite a few settler clearings. The farther north they went, the more inhabited clearings they would encounter.

Where they made a wide sashay before coming back on course, Davy told Jesse they undoubtedly had scouts out who had seen the settlement nearest the Crockett place.

With the sun descending, the trail began to change again, this time bearing more easterly. Jesse thought the reason for this was because in that direction the forests were thick. A large war party could pass along undetected.

Jesse made one of his laconic observations. "Where in hell are them neighbors of your'n?"

Davy had no idea. "They maybe went south. They'd know about them people gettin' killed down there."

Jesse jettisoned his cud, cleared his pipes, and said: "You're a Christian man?"

Davy nodded.

"Well, Davy, it come to me back yonder there must be an easier way to serve the Lord than settlin' in this country."

They stopped where the renegades had halted, read sign, and Davy's worry was strengthened. The renegades were no more than a couple of miles from his clearing. In another hour or so they would see the cabin.

Jesse speculated about the halt. "They counseled. That don't make much sense. All they got to do is keep ridin'. They'll see farms."

Davy dismounted and led his horse. Tracking in a forest was difficult at best, and except that there were so many mounted Indians who trampled undergrowth and small trees, it would have been harder than it was. It did not help that as the sun descended the forest's gloom deepened. They had faced this same situation the night before but this time Davy had the best of all reasons to keep going. His family, the families of his neighbors, even their settlement, were in the worst kind of danger.

Jesse walked behind Davy. Most of the trail was in territory where timber growth made it impossible for men to ride abreast. The men they were trailing had this same difficulty, but, as they spread out, they made the tracking easier.

Jesse was letting his horse drink at a muddied creek when he mentioned food. Davy said: "In the morning. One way or another we'll find it. From them renegades or from some settler." Jesse had to settle for molasses-cured tobacco but his twist was getting shorter since he had been sharing it with Davy, and, while it helped to appease a shrunken stomach, the best chew in the world was no substitute for food.

Forest shadows deepened. Eventually they had to do as they had done the previous night, read sign that was nearly invisible.

The farther they went, the more Davy worried. As often as not renegades attacked after nightfall, particularly if a cabin was so isolated that gunshots would not be heard for any distance. His cabin was such a place.

He and Jesse tracked, listened, and, because the ground was covered inches deep with ancient leaves, even their horses made very little noise.

The trail abruptly veered eastward. Davy sighed with relief. The nearest settler in that direction was a good ten miles distant.

The renegades would not be there until dawn. Jesse loosened the cinch of his horse, let it pick grass where it found any. Davy eventually left his animal with Jesse while he scouted ahead on foot.

He moved like a wraith, had gone more than a mile when he heard talking, this time in English. He crept closer, saw the little cooking fire, and saw something that made the hair on the back of his neck stand straight up.

Three white men were sitting with the Indians, one of whom was Charley Ben. Two of them were bearded men in buckskin. The third man wore a smoke-tanned, fringed buckskin coat and a dark beaver hat. His trousers were worn inside high black boots. Davy could not hear what this man was saying but he could interpret the *wibluta*, sign talk, of one of his bearded companions and was impressed with this man's ability to use sign language. He missed some of it because the firelight was not bright enough to reach very far, but what he understood froze him in his tracks. By sign language the bearded frontiersman was telling the renegades that three Army supply wagons were coming south on the only road going in that direction from the north.

He signed that two of the wagons carried supplies for soldier forts farther south, and the third wagon carried rifles, ammunition, and powder. This wagon was also carrying detonating charges of explosives inside small round objects that had a fuse. When they were thrown after the fuse was lighted, they sent pieces of steel in all directions. The sign-talker only faltered when the white man in the beaver hat explained that these little hand bombs had been imported from France. Since the Indians had no idea where France was, or for that matter what it was, the bearded man gave up and spoke to the stranger in the beaver hat. Davy had been unable to hear what was being said until the other man addressed the Indians in English. He spoke loudly as though by raising his voice those who did not understand or who barely understood English would understand.

He cupped his hands. "Little bombs!" he exclaimed, and used an upright finger to indicate a fuse, then the motion of lighting a sulphur match, holding it to the fuse, drawing his arm back, and making a throwing motion.

Charley Ben seemed to comprehend. He mimicked the other man's gestures and was rewarded with a wide smile and a vigorous nod.

Charley Ben turned to his Indians, spoke rapidly, and again imitated the throwing of a bomb.

Charley Ben then said: "When wagons come?"

The beaver-hatted man answered shortly. "Tomorrow before sundown. They will pass the white rock."

Charley Ben had another question. "Soldiers?"

"Yes. A company of soldiers on horses. You had no trouble finding us. All you do now is ride to the edge of the road where the white rock is. Be ready when they come along."

Davy went back where Jesse and the horses were waiting, told Jesse what he had heard, and Jesse said: "That's why they cut off easterly. They wasn't huntin' places to raid. They went to a meetin' near a white rock with them strangers."

Davy snugged up the girth on his horse, mounted, and told Jesse one of them had to find the settlers and bring them to the roadway.

Jesse agreed to make the search but was not hopeful.

Davy struck out northward to find the wagons and give the warning. As he passed through darkness deep in the forest, he thought about hand bombs. He'd never heard of such things, but if the renegades got them, they wouldn't have to ride into clearings; they could creep up by stealth and hurl the little bombs. They could also use them in ambushes.

CHAPTER
EIGHT

Danger

Davy rode steadily but without haste. He and his horse shared one discomfort: neither had eaten lately.

Darkness increased as he worked his way through the forest. He probably could have gone easterly a mile and used the road, but one thing he had learned back yonder was that Charley Ben's raiders kept scouts out. They wouldn't have to see him; they could hear him. Indians and hound dogs had one thing in common. They could hear leaves stirring.

He had no idea how much time had passed until the chill arrived, which meant dawn was close.

He halted once in a small clearing where a cabin had once stood. All that remained was black char and a lonely stone fireplace.

His horse tugged at the reins so Davy let him have his head. There was a root cellar some distance from where the cabin had stood. Davy got down, flung aside tree branches, found the door, and raised it. Inside, rats scuttled and an aroma of fermentation arose. It was dark in the cellar and warm.

With no way to make fire, Davy groped until he found a corncrib. The ears were as hard as rock, but he took an armload outside and patiently held them for the horse to eat. When he was ready to depart, he looped the reins and worried kernels off the cobs until some of his hunger was appeased.

The cold increased and the sky paled to a uniform sickly blue-gray. He estimated the distance he had traveled, thought he was far enough northward, and angled closer to the road. There was always the danger of scouts but it seemed unlikely they would be this far upcountry.

After daybreak he made a dry camp, fed the horse the last three ears of corn, left the animal tethered, took Betsy, and scouted. Once, from a thin verge where trees had been cut, he saw a farmed clearing in the distance. There was smoke rising from the mud-wattle chimney of a cabin.

He made a wide scout and returned to the horse that was standing, hip-shot, sound asleep.

When he continued northward, he saw sign of many boot tracks. He did not see the men who had made those marks but saw the place where they crossed the road and disappeared into the forest on the east side.

Indians hadn't made those tracks, but red men weren't the only renegades. The entire area for hundreds of miles in most directions was without law. There were few forts and only occasional soldier patrols. Nothing short of a full-fledged army could stop the killing, the peril, and the lawlessness of a countryside in turmoil after the Creek War. There were dozens of villages but few towns. Villages were attacked by large bands of displaced, homeless Indians. The roads were unsafe. Renegade whites rode in deadly bands, better armed than Indians and usually more successful at attacking isolated homesteads and villages because a white man could ride across a clearing in plain sight where an Indian could not.

Davy did not draw rein again until he paused at a creek to tank up the horse. Here, the sign was fresh and had been made by moccasins. He tied the horse and followed the tracks. There were two of them; one had small feet. That would be a woman.

He found the horses before he found their owners. One of them was indeed a woman. Her companion was young, muscular, and well-armed. They were eating cold meat within a short distance of the creek.

The buck had a knife and hatchet. His rifle was leaning close where creek willows flourished.

Davy did not step into sight and did not raise his voice when he said: "If you got food to spare, I sure could use it."

The woman froze. The Indian sat, straight and motionless, for seconds before turning to look in the direction of Davy's voice.

Davy came around a tree, rifle in the crook of one arm. He said — "Name's Crockett." — and walked toward the Indians.

As he hunkered, the woman passed him some cold meat. She was expressionless. She was also young and pretty. Her companion was a Creek. He watched Davy wolf down food and finally spoke. "You alone?"

Davy nodded as he reached for more meat.

The Indians exchanged a glance before the Creek spoke again. "Why are you out here?"

Davy drew a buckskin cuff across his lips before replying. "Hunting," he said. "You, too?"

The Indian, wary but curious, shook his head. "Hunt to eat," he stated. "We go north. Too much trouble here. Too many enemies."

Davy relaxed and gazed at the buck. "Friend, if you go north, you're going to run into more white skins than you can shake a stick at an' they ain't fond of Indians."

"We at peace," the Indian said, and again Davy shook his head. "Maybe you are but most other folks ain't. Indians or whites."

The Indian looked at his woman. She looked back in silence, but had the same thought. He addressed Davy again. "Can't go east. Choctaws on war trail. Can't go south, all full of settlers."

"Go west," Davy said. "Keep goin' west until there ain't no settlers, no soldiers. Many miles, the farther you go the better."

The Indian did an odd thing. He produced a twist of Kentucky-cured tobacco from his parfleche and held it out. Davy accepted the tobacco, bit off a corner, and handed it back. He had known very few Indians who chewed tobacco. The buck put the twist back into its pouch without taking a chew. He said: "A band of white raiders crossed the road miles back going toward Creek country."

Davy nodded. "I saw their sign."

The Indian said: "Muller."

Davy had heard of a renegade band headed by a white man named Muller but had never met the man or his raiders. Muller's reputation, though, was bad. The Indian held up both hands, fingers extended, then lowered one hand, and again raised all five fingers of the other hand.

Davy thought that was about right. The sign he'd read back yonder had been made by about fifteen riders crossing the road.

Davy thanked the Indian for the food, went back to his horse, and continued riding northward. As he rode, he remembered stories he'd heard about the Muller raiders; they were grisly. He wondered why Muller would be heading into Creek country, which was now full of displaced Indians on the move, and soldiers. Anyone riding in that kind of country would be running a high risk.

The sun did not burn through the treetops but there was welcome new-day warmth. When he thought he might be in the area where the Army wagons were coming south, he angled over close enough to be able to see the roadway. He stopped several times to listen, heard no wagons, and continued northward until a flock of wild pigeons flew frantically overhead on a southwesterly course.

He heard something that had nothing to do with wagons. A wild turkey gobbled loudly on the east side of the road and was answered by another turkey on the west side. The last turkey sounded close to the area Davy was riding through.

He hid the horse in a dense stand of timber and brush, waited briefly for either of those turkeys to sound again, and, when neither did, he began a stalk.

The sound of the bird on the west side of the road had been deeper in the forest.

Both calls had been perfect imitations, but when one tom turkey gobbled it was unlikely another would do the same from a distance.

He could be wrong, but he possessed something only frontiersmen developed — if they lived long enough — instinct.

He reached the area where the second turkey had called, moving cautiously from tree to tree.

Any time of year forests had birds, particularly in the spring and summer. Davy neither saw nor heard birds. When the little bell in the back of his mind was ringing an alarm, he crouched in a large thicket. A short man in stained buckskins who had a full beard was standing with his back to Davy's bush. The distance was not great but it was great enough so that, if Davy came out of his bushes to attack, the other man would hear the noise and whirl before Davy could reach him. He could not use his rifle. If there was one man, there might be others. He had his knife and hatchet, but, although he was a dead shot with Betsy, he had never mastered the art of throwing a tomahawk or a knife.

While he watched, the bearded man turned in the direction of the road and disappeared among the trees.

Davy thought the man had been a scout. He had not seen or heard other men. Scouts ranged ahead on both sides of moving bands, which meant the main body of men was deeper in the forest to the west or north.

He waited a long time in his place of concealment before rising up. There was no sign of the bearded man and there was not a sound; particularly there were no birds.

Davy left his bush, moving from cover to cover on a westerly course. If the other men were northward, he wanted to make certain they would not be behind him as he moved upcountry.

He did not speculate on their reason for being here. He concentrated on finding them — if they were close by — but the bearded men in buckskins could have also been alone, as Davy was.

He hadn't covered more than a quarter mile before he detected a familiar scent — pipe smoke.

He hid again in underbrush, trying to correct his stalk in the proper direction, but the scent was too faint for that. It did, however, settle the question of other men hiding in the forest.

The day was waning. It was still hot with high humidity, and, although there would still be several hours of daylight in open country, in the forest the gloom deepened.

Davy wondered about the Army wagons and their dragoon escort. Until he knew where the men were he was stalking, he dared not continue northward to intercept the wagons. That bearded man who had gone in the direction of the trees would see anyone near the road.

A horse nickered. The sound, though soft, was followed by loud profanity and the sharp sound of someone using a whip.

Davy was finally able to set the direction and moved westward as he also yielded ground southward.

After what had happened at Charley Ben's encampment when he and Jesse had been caught flat-footed, he occasionally looked back. Somewhere, not too distant, was that bearded man, probably closer to the road, but that was nothing Davy cared to bet his life on.

He did not see the men. He saw tethered horses impatiently fidgeting. He did not count them as he moved with extreme caution among the trees and brush, helped by the increasing gloom.

The first man he saw had a brace of pistols in his belt. He was unwashed, unshorn, and lean. He was smoking a little pipe.

Davy hunkered in a big bush, counted fourteen men. One man in particular caught his attention. He wore a red sash that had a brace of pistols in it. His knife sheath was elaborately beaded. Dangling from the sheath's bottom was a small circlet of twigs in the center of which was a small scalp lock dried hard and held inside the circlet by rawhide strips. Aside from the flamboyant sash what caught Davy's attention was the way this man took snuff from a small silver box and sniffed it. Red Sash and the others were white men; there was not an Indian among them. *They could not be Charley Ben's Choctaw renegades.*

Red Sash was broad-shouldered and thick-chested but was not very tall. He had jet-black hair and his skin was weathered darker than was customary.

Davy speculated that he might be some kind of half-breed Indian. If so, he was the only frontiersman Davy had seen who wore a red sash.

Several of the men were eating. The pipe smoker said something to Red Sash and got an answer Davy could not hear. The pipe smoker disappeared eastward through the forest. He could have been sent to relieve the bearded scout near the road, or to join him. Either way there were now two men far enough eastward to be between Davy and his horse.

A coarse-featured individual who was wiping grease off his fingers on his trousers called to Red Sash. "They should've been here by now. It'll be dark directly."

He got no reply. Red Sash was standing with his head cocked. Eventually he faced around and spoke sharply. "Mount up."

There was a scramble as men got to their feet, sheathed the knives they had used as eating utensils, and without a word went out where the horses were. Red Sash was the last man astride. As he swung over leather, he said: "Did you hear it? The turkey gobbled."

Davy used the time the men got mounted to slip out of his hiding place and move in the direction of the road. He did not worry about being detected by mounted men following Red Sash. The gloom had increased the last hour. If Davy had stood up in plain sight, as long as he didn't move, they wouldn't have seen him.

He got back to his horse, mounted, and rode northward within shouting distance of the hastily abandoned camp. There was no one there, just some cast asides.

If Red Sash had been signaled, something was coming southward on the road. Davy had to get far enough northward to warn of an ambush.

This time he pushed the horse that could travel no faster than a rapid walk because of trees and increasingly poor visibility, but he did pick up the gait a little.

Eventually Davy edged closer to the road, running the risk of detection, but he had to find the wagons before they were ambushed.

He heard nothing as he hastened, until he topped out over a rib of land that went as far as the road and across it. This rise created a natural bulwark in the otherwise flat course of the road.

Davy reached it in the forest, and followed its easterly course in the direction of the road. When he could make out the road through forest gloom, he again tied the horse, took his rifle, and went ahead on foot. When he reached the final fringe of trees, he stopped. This time he heard wagons, still distant but grinding steadily southward.

A turkey gobbled loudly to the south. Davy guessed the call had been made by either the bearded man or the pipe smoker. If so, they were moving upcountry in his direction.

Davy hid and waited. The first man he saw was neither of the scouts. It was a tall Indian, standing motionlessly beside a tree. He was peering in the direction of the gobbler's call.

Davy did not think this Indian was part of the raider band. There hadn't been an Indian among them. He understood the Indian's anxiety. Turkeys roosted at dusk; they didn't gobble.

The Indian hooked his rifle into the crook of one arm and began moving westerly — deeper into the forest. Davy guessed the Indian had no idea there were men hiding close by, but whatever he thought, hurrying westward was the prudent direction for someone who did not want to be seen.

A night-hunting owl swept through the trees with uncanny ability until Davy moved. The owl detected movement and furiously beat silent wings to get clear.

Again the turkey gobbled. It was difficult to see any distance into the forest, but this turkey was coming toward the road using the same land swell Davy had used.

The sound of wagons was closer and more distinct. Davy found a large old deadfall, got on the north side of it, and hoped the oncoming scout would be southward.

He watched intently for shadowy motion. If they were together — pipe smoker and whiskers — Davy was not in the best position of his life.

He settled Betsy atop the big old deadfall tree and waited.

The sound of oncoming wagons was now loud enough for Davy to be able to discern the sound of shod horses with the wagons.

CHAPTER
NINE

Stalemate

Davy had a choice — run to the road and signal for the cavalcade to halt, or lie behind this deadfall tree until the renegade scouts appeared. The decision was made for him when the bear-built scout appeared out of the gloom. If Davy jumped up and raced toward the road, a renegade could easily shoot him in the back.

The second scout appeared. They halted, facing in the direction of the road where wagon sounds were clearly audible even through the forest.

Davy was not going to be able to reach the road but he had an opportunity to do something that might provide a warning to the wagoners and their soldier escort.

He settled Betsy atop the deadfall, took careful aim, and fired. Pipe Smoker's old leather hat took wing like a wounded bird and disappeared among the trees. Both scouts dropped. One said — "Yonder's the smoke." — and fired his rifle. It was a clean miss. As this scout settled around to reload, his hatless companion took long aim, which provided Davy with enough time to roll clear so that when the musket ball struck punky wood the man who had shot from behind the log was two yards away.

There were startled shouts from the roadway, but Davy's warning had brought other renegades in an angry rush.

They had been anticipating a successful ambush since the previous evening, and, although they had no idea who had fired the first shot, they wanted to find him. He had destroyed their element of surprise.

Davy had no time to reload. He scuttled northward until he had sufficient forest cover, then got to his feet and ran, dodging around trees, heading for the roadway, fully aware of the danger. Renegades would be ahead where they had infiltrated the forest.

He was swerving to avoid a big wood rat's nest when a man on the far side shoved out his leg. Davy saw the obstacle too late.

As he fell, the renegade scrambled to his feet and leaped with his sheath knife raised. Davy rolled, fetched up against a large rock and so could roll no farther, and swung his rifle. The renegade took the blow in the middle and briefly staggered. Before Davy could get clear of the boulder, the renegade jumped at him, slashing with his knife.

Davy felt the cut. It was as if he'd been branded with a hot iron. He closed with the knife wielder, who was a tall, sinewy individual with pale eyes and a gash for a mouth.

Davy blocked the descending knife hand, rolled the man half over, and straddled him. His antagonist was strong. The knife had been halted in the air but its descent seemed inexorable regardless of how hard Davy fought to stop it.

The renegade's breath hissed out as he fought to dislodge Davy. Cords stood out in his neck. Davy struck the renegade with his fist. He might as well have struck rock. The renegade blinked and fought like a tiger. Davy leaned, got his forearm across the man's throat, and bore down as hard as he could.

The renegade continued to struggle right up until his eyes bulged and the knife-wielding arm began to falter.

Davy leaned harder, using all his upper body weight to cut off the air the renegade was trying to inhale. When the knife arm loosened, Davy let go of the man's wrist, turned his head until they were eye to eye, then hit the man in the side of the head as hard as he could. The renegade briefly arched before turning loose all over.

Davy got to his feet, sucking air, picked up his rifle, and pushed ahead in the direction of the road.

He wanted to sit down and catch his breath but kept going and was almost to the road when a rattle of musket fire made him stop.

Someone yelled. Davy could see the halted wagons and several of the soldiers. Others were either coming into the forest or were on the far side of the wagons.

One teamster was standing on the offside of his team to prevent a stampede. As far as Davy could see, this man was armed with a belt knife. He was an easy target despite the fidgeting and lunging panic of his horses. There was abrupt gunfire behind Davy, a couple of yells, and more gunfire. Evidently the soldiers had infiltrated the gloom where dusk was settling although it was still daylight in the roadway.

What had bothered him from his first sighting of the encamped renegades bothered him now. The freighters, soldiers, and renegades were not only behind Davy; they were also between him and his horse.

He watched for movement in order to be sufficiently forewarned to glide around his tree if someone came his way, but, when it eventually happened, it was four men sweeping toward the deeper forest, two on each side of Davy's tree.

He dropped flat and scarcely breathed, but the soldiers were looking ahead, not down or close by. Every time there was a gunshot, they pushed ahead seeking targets with rifles held at the ready in both hands.

After they passed, Davy got to his feet, brushed off dirt and leaves, and moved cautiously in the direction of the road where teamsters and a wounded soldier were on the far side of the wagons.

The horses were still in place, which they probably would not have been if that teamster hadn't kept his lead team from stampeding. Now, as the fight continued westerly in the forest's settling dusk, Davy reached the edge of the trees beside the road and called out.

"My name's Crockett. I fired off the first round to warn you they were waitin' to ambush you. You hear me?"

He got an answer but it was a long time coming. "What do you want an' who's with you?"

"Ain't nobody with me. Hold your fire. I'm comin' out."

He saw gun barrels beneath the first wagon as he moved down to the roadbed, halted, and leaned on his rifle. "You gents satisfied?"

This time the answer ignored the question. "Walk over here an' lean your rifle on a wagon wheel."

Davy obeyed, leaned Betsy where he'd been told to, and waited until a white-faced, hatless man wearing a blue uniform came into view, holding a cocked pistol in his left hand. His right arm wore a bloody bandage and was tucked inside his tunic. This man looked long in the direction from which Davy had come until Davy said: "I told you I came alone. You got some whiskey?"

A peevish-sounding voice came from the tailgate end of the first wagon. "It's Crockett for a fact, Lieutenant. I seen him at half a dozen shootin' matches. I'll get the whiskey."

The officer was still not satisfied about the man in buckskin who had appeared out of the forest and whose sleeve was torn and stained with blood. He led the way behind the first wagon where a wounded man was lying on some blankets. There were four of them, five counting Davy whose presence was welcomed by only one of them, a thin, stooped older man who offered a bottle to Davy as he said: "You're a far piece from home, ain't you?"

Davy swallowed twice, handed the bottle back, and nodded. "I heard about the wagons coming from some raiders I eavesdropped on in the woods."

The officer asked who the renegades were. All Davy could tell him was their numbers and that their leader wore a red sash.

106

The officer pointed toward some cloth and liniment. "Cain'll bandage it for you. A red sash?"

"Yes."

"Short, dark fellow with a scalp lock on his knife sheath?"

"That's him. Who is he?"

"His name is Breaux."

"Breaux? That ain't Indian."

"It's a long story. He's from French Canada an' fought against us with the British. After the war he went to raidin' and plunderin'. The government's got a bounty on him. One hundred dollars."

Davy's eyes widened. In his country a man did not make that much in a year. "Ain't he a long way from home?"

The officer made a sour smile. "He's wherever he shows up. The Army's been after him since the war."

"You carryin' guns an' powder in them wagons?"

This time the lieutenant looked steadily at Davy a long time before nodding curtly without speaking.

Davy said: "An' some little bombs a man throws after lighting a fuse?"

This time the officer's stare was unwavering. "Where did you hear that?" he demanded.

"From three white men who met some renegades. One of them wore a mighty fine beaver hat an' a long buckskin coat."

The officer nodded when the stooped, wiry man came up with a bottle and some bandaging cloth. "Give him another drink," he told the raffish older man. "I've got to find out where they went in the forest."

As the officer was turning away, Davy dryly said: "If you find them soldiers, you better get 'em back here. Renegades are natural ambushers."

He watched the officer cross the road toward the trees. Cain, the old teamster, went to work on the wound as he said: "He ain't as stiff as he acts. This ruckus caught him dozin' in the saddle. He's new to this part of the country."

Davy saw the lieutenant disappear and said: "He shouldn't have let them soldiers go scattering in the forest."

The old man worked in silence. When he was finished, he made a little clucking sound. "Ruined a good shirt, but, if he'd aimed a tad to the right, you wouldn't care about no shirt. Come along. That ain't the only bottle we brung along."

Davy went with the old man. One of the other teamsters had a bottle. After they'd all had a swallow, Davy said: "That officer'll get himself shot. Don't you have a bugler along?"

One of the teamsters pointed to the pallet where the wounded man was lying. "He's the bugler."

There was an occasional random shot. Otherwise the forest was quiet. Davy shook his head. He'd seen his share of officers but never any who'd leave wagons unguarded.

The fighting seemed to be diminishing as an occasional gunshot sounded southward. Davy was fed some cold beans and deer meat. He thought that the lieutenant must be as green as grass, not just for going into the forest with only a sword, but for not concentrating his soldiers around the wagons. Three teamsters, their swampers, and a wounded bugler would be no help if the wagons were attacked, and it was the wagons the renegades wanted.

Daylight was fading. Cain, as lead teamster, worried about the horses. He told the other drivers to grain the animals. He told Davy, if the lieutenant didn't return directly, he was going to continue southward. He did not like the notion of being a sitting duck in the middle of the road.

The lieutenant returned with seven soldiers, all he could find. He was in a foul mood. When he saw Davy cleaning and reloading Betsy, he asked if there was any way to find men who would ride with the wagons.

Davy tipped in powder and stoppered the horn before answering. "A friend of mine went looking for some fellers. I got no idea where he is, whether he found 'em, or where they are, but except for them there ain't no more until you get to the next settlement. An' if you struck out right now, you wouldn't reach no settlement until morning." Davy leaned on his recharged weapon. He was half a head taller than the lieutenant. "I'll tell you what I figure."

"I'm listening, Mister Crockett."

"I think the feller with the fancy sash is leading them soldiers you didn't find as far off as he can."

"They're veterans, Mister Crockett. They can take care of themselves."

"That's likely," Davy said. "That ain't what troubles me. If that feller with the red bellyband's as smart as

I'm beginning to figure he is, he ain't through with you. Not yet, Lieutenant."

Several teamsters had drifted up to listen, old Cain among them. He said: "Spit it out, Davy."

"Whether you get moving or camp here in the road for the night, the red-sash feller's going to hit you again. There's another band of renegades, mostly Choctaws. They're with that feller I told you talked to that feller with the fancy hat. His name's Charley Ben. I got no idea how he knew where to meet the feller with the beaver hat, but they sure enough met, an' Fancy Hat told Charley Ben about them little bombs. That's where I heard about them. Charley Ben's coming upcountry, too. If them two bands meet, by my count that'll make about forty renegades. How many soldiers you got?"

There was not a sound among the teamsters until the lieutenant said twenty, then one of the teamsters snorted: "You got seven here, Lieutenant, an' one shot, lyin' on some blankets. Where's the rest of 'em? You sent 'em into them trees, that's where they are."

Before the lieutenant could answer there was a deafening bugle blast. They all looked around. The wounded man was sitting up, supported by a teamster. He had blasted out the call for retreat. Afterward the teamster eased him back down.

Davy went over to the pallet. The wounded man was very young. He had been hit in the upper right leg, and, although he had been cared for, blood showed through the bandaging. Davy called for whiskey, knelt, held the bugler's head up until he had swallowed three times,

110

then eased him back down. The bugler broke out into a sweat and smiled at Davy.

The officer came up frowning. "Who told you to sound retreat?" he demanded.

Whiskey worked fast on an empty stomach. The youth's eyes held to the officer's face as he replied: "The angel Gabriel, sir."

Nine soldiers emerged from the forest, dirty, sweaty, and strongly silent as they reached the wagons. The officer asked if they had seen others, and a grizzled man with coarse features and a hostile stare answered gruffly: "Two missin'. Them renegades kept ahead until they could get around us in the timber."

The old teamster named Cain made a blunt statement. "Ambushed you boys. You'd ought to have your damned heads examined for goin' in there with daylight fadin'."

The lieutenant turned, red-faced, toward the old man. Before he could speak, Davy said: "Lieutenant, it'll be dark directly. If you set here in the road, they'll have your hair by morning."

The angry officer answered defiantly: "We'll protect the wagons, Mister Crockett. That's what we were sent to do."

Davy considered the officer in silence for a moment. He had met officers he had thought deserved to be shot, but this one took the rag off the bush for being stubborn. He was as stubborn as oak and twice as thick in the head.

"Lieutenant, them Choctaws will reach here directly. Whether they hitch horses with your Canadian or not, have you any idea what the odds are going to be?" Davy leaned on his rifle, looking steadily at the officer. "About the same as the devil chasing a crippled saint."

Two limping soldiers came out of the forest to the road. One had lost his rifle; the other one was using his weapon as a crutch. They came up in silence. One had been grazed across the shoulder; the other one had been hit in the lower leg. The teamsters took them away to be cared for. The others went with them, leaving the lieutenant and Davy alone.

Davy wagged his head. "Mister, except that they want rifles, powder, an' them little bombs, they'd shoot into the wagons, an' blow 'em up."

The officer watched as someone lighted a small lantern back where the wounded soldiers were being cared for. When he returned his attention to Crockett, he said: "We'll get to moving."

Davy turned aside to expectorate before speaking. "You'll be like setting ducks on a pond. By now I'd guess they're on both sides of the road."

"We could turn back, fight a withdrawing action, Mister Crockett."

Davy blew out a ragged breath. Twice as thick as oak had been an underestimation. "Mister, it doesn't matter which way you go or if you don't move at all. By now . . ." Davy turned and raised his voice. "Blow out that light!" The lantern was snuffed. Davy finished what he had been saying to the lieutenant: "Go or set still, when they're ready, they'll attack. My guess is that Mister Breaux's raiders have to be all collected after your soldiers scattered 'em. When he's ready, he'll attack from both sides of the road. An' if them Choctaws come up, or if they're close enough to hear gunfire, they'll pile into you, too."

The lieutenant's expression reflected his inner foreboding. This was his first critical assignment. He turned slightly to regard the wagons and shadowy shapes among them.

Davy watched the officer; in the poor light he seemed to have aged. When he faced forward, Davy said: "Caught like a rat in a snap trap. What I learned in the Creek War was that defending yourself ain't as good as offending someone else."

The officer nodded slightly. "That's why I sent the soldiers into the forest. The best defense is offense."

"For a fact, Lieutenant, but only if you've got a chance, which you didn't have during daylight an' which you don't have now."

"I'll blow up the wagons!"

"I got a notion, Lieutenant."

"It better be a miracle, Mister Crockett."

"Lend me that teamster named Cain, give him a rifle, a hatchet, an' a knife if he don't have one, an' ask him to meet me here."

The officer did not appear heartened, but he was curious. "I'll send him. What do you figure to do?"

"We can talk later. I'd take it kindly if you send me that teamster."

The lieutenant hesitated briefly, then went after the man named Cain. When the teamster appeared where Davy was leaning against a wagon wheel with a fresh cud of Kentucky twist in his cheek, the lieutenant was with him. Davy offered Cain some chewing tobacco that the old man accepted, but, when the same offer was made to the officer, he shook his head. He was waiting for Davy to speak, which Davy did, but not to the officer, rather to the old man. "You ever scouted, Mister Cain?"

"Well, only to hunt."

"You scairt of Indians or renegades?"

"Yes, I'm scairt of 'em. I'd be a damned fool not to be."

Davy smiled. "Let's you 'n' me see if we can both get scairt. Lieutenant . . ."

"I'd like to know what you got in mind, Mister Crockett."

"I've got in mind seeing if I can get that miracle for you. Let's go Mister Cain."

They left the officer standing by the fore wheel, passed from sight the moment they reached the easterly forest, and somewhere a considerable distance southward an owl hooted.

CHAPTER
TEN

The Wagon Fight

There was a puny moon, cocked up at both ends. It was the kind folks said meant rain because a man could hang his powder horn on it and it wouldn't fall off.

Davy moved stealthily until he came to a thick stand of trees with underbrush. He had no illusions of them being alone. Whether Red Sash's entire party was on the east side of the road or not, there certainly would be spies watching the wagons.

Cain shifted his shot pouch and that made the musket balls rattle. It wasn't much of a sound but Davy scowled. Cain looked more embarrassed than apologetic.

Davy made a hooting sound. When the response came, it wasn't an owl; it was the mournful call of a nightbird. Davy led off in that direction as soundless as a ghost. The old man followed, having to work at suppressing his fear.

Without warning, a buckskin wraith appeared in front of them as though he'd come out of the ground. He softly said: "Enos?"

Davy answered in a loud whisper: "Where's the others?"

The dimly discernible ghost answered shortly. "Close around. Did you see the soldier with his arm inside his coat come back with them two crippled ones?"

Davy took two steps closer to the wraith as he answered: "What's Breaux waitin' for?"

The discernible man leaned on his rifle as he replied: "For them boys that led the soldiers south to get back."

Davy halted. He could not see the man well, just his outline and it blended with his surroundings. "Breaux across the road?" he asked.

It was the wrong question. The buckskin ghost did not reply; he began to straighten up from his slouched stance. Davy held his rifle low in both hands. He cocked the gun. It made the kind of sound once heard was never forgotten, but in the forest it did not carry far.

Davy spoke to the old man behind him. "Get his rifle, Mister Cain."

The old man moved cautiously around Davy. He did not act as though this situation was something he enjoyed, which it wasn't. After thirty years as a teamster he was, as he had said before he and Davy reached the forest, scared of Indians and renegades. But he had sense enough to approach the renegade to one side, not directly in front, which would have blocked Davy's view.

The renegade relinquished his rifle without looking at the old man. As Cain took the man's hatchet and knife, Davy moved closer. The renegade said: "Crockett."

Davy nodded. "You got a name?"

"Jackson."

"President Jackson?"

The renegade showed worn-down teeth in a cold smile. "None other."

Davy motioned with his rifle. "Lie down, President Jackson."

As the renegade moved to obey, he said: "You 'n' them soldiers won't be around come daylight."

Davy's answer was directed toward the old man. "Tie his arms in back. Use his belt to bind his ankles. Do it, Mister Cain. Take the thong offen his powder horn. Tie his hands in back real good."

As the old man put the weapons aside to kneel, the renegade looked up at Davy, wearing that same wolfish small smile. "You know how many of us there are?"

"About twenty."

"Then use your head. Set me loose an' join us. We'll take them wagons when the screech owl hoots."

Davy watched Cain do his work. When the old man arose, Davy moved close, swung the butt plate of his rifle, and at the horrified look he got from the old man he explained: "He'll sleep for a spell. When he comes around, he'll yell. We've got to be gone when he does that."

They made their way ahead, halted once when they heard two men arguing, made a wide sashay around that place, and continued easterly until Davy finally halted near a rough-barked old tree. He gave the old man time to rest before striking out again, but this time due southward.

Not a word passed between them. If Cain was troubled by their change of course, he said nothing. Davy still moved with caution, but, although he was certain the forest on both sides of the road was inhabited by enemies, what he had in mind required risk, and haste.

The next time they halted, the old man got a fresh cud of Kentucky twist into his cheek and sat on a wind-downed log. Davy stood, listening. The only sound was of running water somewhere eastward. When they resumed their walk, Davy went farther south, half a mile or so, then changed course again, this time going westerly toward the road. Cain followed without a sound.

The road looked gray as a corpse in the night. Davy pressed as far as the final fringe of forest, halted, leaned on his rifle for a long few moments, then jerked his head, and walked out to the road, crossed it, and kept moving until they were in more darkness with trees around them again. Twice he halted to listen, and twice he angled slightly southward until the last time he halted.

Cain's heart was beating fast. He jettisoned his cud and started to speak. Davy held up a hand for silence. The old man strained to detect sound and failed. Davy leaned and said: "They didn't make as good time as I figured they would."

Because it was difficult to see, Davy moved slowly and cautiously. After some time he halted again, and this time the old man heard what sounded like men

118

speaking in short bursts in a language he did not understand. He whispered to Davy: "Indians?"

Davy nodded, put his finger to his lips, and led off warily.

When they were closer and the sounds were louder, Davy suddenly stopped in mid-stride. Cain almost bumped him. He moved around where he could see Indians standing around a saddled horse. Davy leaned to whisper again. "They found my critter."

The Indians spoke gutturally. One man asked a question in English. "Where is he?"

The answer came from a dark, sullen-faced Indian. "Maybe it is Beaver Hat's horse."

That brought a comment from another Indian. "Beaver Hat went west to the settler town."

"Maybe it is a hunter's horse."

That brought a derisive answer. "Horse been tied a long time. Hunter wouldn't leave horse."

There was more speculation. Davy waited until he had heard enough to understand that what had delayed Charley Ben's raiders had been this unexplainable mystery of a saddled horse tied to a tree in the forest with no one around.

He took Cain deeper into the forest, found a place of concealment, and said: "How good a shot are you, Mister Cain?"

As with all frontiersmen this question impinged on a man's pride. "Good enough. Fair to middlin'. You ain't crazy enough to fight all them Indians, I hope."

Davy cocked his head. The Indians were arguing, by this time loudly. Cain frowned at his companion: "I know you're a crack shot. I've heard stories of your shooting, but there's at least fifteen, twenty buck Indians back there."

Davy waited until the argument diminished, then said: "How good a runner are you?"

The old man set his back to a tree and spoke sharply when he replied: "I'm seventy-four years old. When I was forty years younger, I couldn't outrun no twenty fightin' Indians. We'd best just go back an' leave them tomahawks alone."

Davy jerked his head northward as he said: "You start running. I'll catch up. But be right careful because Red Sash's men ain't more'n a mile upcountry."

"What're you goin' to do?" the old man asked.

"When you hear a rifle shot, stop an' I'll be along."

Cain looked straight at Crockett. "You're crazier'n a pet 'coon," he said, picked up his rifle, and walked northward.

Davy's last words to him were: "Run, don't walk. Run."

The old man broke into a run, and, although he went up and down a lot, he didn't really cover much ground.

Davy waited until he could neither see nor hear the old man, then stalked the Indian camp. His horse had been tied where there was tall grass and was eating as though he hadn't done that in quite a while, which he hadn't.

The Indians were squatting in a rough circle, using knives to cut meat as they ate and talked. Davy missed Jesse, who understood some Indian languages, although maybe not Choctaw.

That derisive Indian who used English told Charley Ben it didn't make much difference whether they attacked the wagons now or waited until dawn when targets were better.

Several others grunted agreement as they ate. One wary buck, who was still spooked about the saddled horse they had found, said: "Maybe wagons got scouts. Maybe horse belonged to one of 'em. Maybe he's scouting us up right now."

The derisive Indian had an answer to that. "Good. He sees how many we got an' tells the soldiers, they'll run back the way they come."

The sullen-faced dark Indian was too busy eating to take part in the discussion. Just once did he growl around a mouthful of meat. He addressed the derisive man. "We get closer and wait. We get within shooting range and wait for light."

The only reason Davy had made his long stalk was so that something like this wouldn't happen. He had sent Cain away because he had wanted to hear what Charley Ben had just said.

He found a tree that suited his purpose, placed Betsy in a crotch, waited until Charley Ben was raising a piece of meat, and fired.

Charley Ben jumped with a howl. The other Indians were too surprised to move for seconds. Davy didn't wait for them to jump up. He ran as swiftly as he could northward, almost ran past where Cain was hiding because he heard noisy and angry pursuit. He paused to yell at the old man to run for his life.

Behind them Indians howled. One or two of them, uncertain where that shot had come from, ran in slightly different directions. One of them went toward the road.

The old man kept up with his longer-legged and younger companion but he was sucking air like a fish out of water by the time Davy veered into a flourishing thicket. Davy told the old man to stay there, and resumed his northward course but no longer running.

Charley Ben's howls were loudest. That musket ball that had knocked the hunk of meat from his hand had also caused his wrist to be violently wrenched. Pain as much as fury drove him.

Davy reloaded his rifle, lengthened his stride, gauged the distance of the pursuing renegades, and broke over into a trot. Visibility was bad, otherwise he might have been hit when a man fired at him from the direction of the road. He ducked behind a tree but could make out neither shape nor movement where the other man would be reloading.

He eased deeper westward, went back for the old man, and took him northward but on an angling westerly course until Cain squawked and grabbed Davy's arm.

The man Cain saw was in the direction of the road, too far eastward to see a pair of wraiths westerly. He was leaning and listening. Charley Ben's Choctaws were still yelling but not as furiously as they had when they had started in pursuit.

Davy pushed the old man to the ground, got down beside him, and waited.

The man who could hear yelling Indians coming toward him turned and yelled through cupped hands. Belatedly he made the cry of a screech owl, the nighttime signal of alarm.

Somewhere southward a gun fired. The ball did not hit the man who had shouted but it caused him to run.

Davy tugged at the old man who resisted, saying: "I want to see this."

Davy lifted him to his feet with one hand and growled: "They'll scatter an' we ain't going to be here when they come."

Cain dutifully followed Davy. They went west for more than a mile, then changed course, went at least that far north, and halted to listen to the fight where Charley Ben's Choctaws had met Red Sash's renegades and were now waging war in a dark forest.

Davy went warily and slowly. When he thought they were far enough northward, he changed course again, and headed directly toward the road.

The fighting did not slacken. Neither side knew who their adversaries were. All they knew was they were being attacked in force. Casualties would be few unless the opponents fought hand to hand. The best sharpshooter on earth could not rely on his accuracy if targets were moving in a forest in the middle of a dark night.

When Davy and the old man came to the final tier of trees bordering the roadway, they were too far upcountry to see wagons, so they skirted southward until they could make that distinction before leaving the forest.

Every man who was able was standing by the wagons with their full attention on the gunfire and shouts not too distant southward on the west side of the road.

Davy and Cain walked toward the tailgate of the last wagon, went around the near side, and almost got shot by three teamsters as jumpy as cats who saw them come from behind the wagon. Cain swore. "Jenks, you half-wit, it's me! Button, aim that gun somewhere else. You danged idiots!"

Davy ignored the startled teamsters, walked down where the lieutenant was standing stiff as a ramrod, and touched his shoulder.

The officer whirled. One of the soldiers said: "I'll be damned. Where's Cain?"

"Back yonder where his friends liked to have shot us. Lieutenant, there's your miracle. Them renegade Indians came onto Red Sash's friends."

The officer was silent for a long time before he said: "You did that?"

"All we did, mister, was get them two bands to find one another. One musket ball got it started."

The old man came up. "Them damned fellers back yonder went an' drunk all the whiskey."

A soldier using his rifle as a crutch so that his bandaged leg wouldn't touch the ground held a bottle toward the old man, who accepted it, swallowed several times, handed back the bottle, and said: "Mister Crockett liked to got me killed." He turned, went toward the first wagon, climbed up, and disappeared under the covering.

The lieutenant listened a while longer to the gunfire before using his uninjured arm to produce a crooked cigar, as black as original sin, and offer it to Davy, who declined.

Several men drifted away. The soldier who had been grazed over the shoulder asked who was fighting Breaux's outlaws. Davy told him about the Choctaws under the Creek called Charley Ben. The soldier then wanted to know how those two bands had got to fighting.

Davy accepted the bottle a man offered, drank deeply, handed back the bottle, and said: "We ain't out of the woods yet. No matter who turns tail first over there, there'll still be the other fellers to worry about."

A teamster gruffly spoke. "At the way they're goin' at it, hammer 'n' tongs, won't be many left."

The gunfire did not slacken for an hour, then it seemed to be scattered, as though the combatants were hunting, stalking one another.

Davy told the lieutenant Charley Ben's Indians most likely wouldn't stop fighting unless they either ran out of ammunition or targets.

The officer looked for something to sit on, found an upended small barrel, sat down, and wagged his head at Davy. "After you left, they told me stories about you, but, Mister Crockett, if you live to be a hundred, I doubt you'll ever do anythin' like this again. When I get home, I'll write in my report how you came up with the only idea that could've saved the wagons."

CHAPTER
ELEVEN

Moving Wagons

The fight did not end for another hour, and, although Davy was restless, he remained with the wagons. After the last shot had been fired, he told the lieutenant it might be a good idea to get the wagons moving. At the protest this brought, Davy said: "Whoever comes out on top ain't going to set down an' lick his wounds. If we set here another day, they'll gather what they ain't lost and hit us as sure as I'm standing here."

The lieutenant said: "At least we can fort up here, an' if we get strung out on the road . . ."

"Mister, you keep the drivers. I'll divvy up what's left, half on one side of the road, other half on the other side. It may not work, but setting here another day will be worse. There's no relief coming. Moving, we got a chance, setting here like ducks on a pond we got no chance."

The injured arm that the lieutenant kept inside his tunic was throbbing, and had been doing so since the day before. The pain was demoralizing.

He looked back where men were standing, shrugged, and called out: "Line 'em out! Cain, you 'n' all but the drivers come up here. Fetch your weapons."

Counting soldiers and swampers there were twelve men able to scout. Davy divided them, six to the easterly woods, six to the west, put Cain in charge of the east side scouts, told the men he would take to the west. They would not penetrate any farther into the forest than he thought there might be ambushers. As he finished speaking, he looked at the officer, who nodded understanding that he would stay with the wagon. Davy said: "Them drivers will be sitting ducks."

The officer nodded. If the drivers could be shot off their high seats, the renegades could take over farther down the road when the horses would not be restrained by strong hands on the lines.

There was nothing the lieutenant could do about this except put a soldier atop each wagon. Two of them were wounded but in a desperate situation they could fight. The only man put inside a wagon was the wounded bugler.

Davy considered Cain. "Be careful," he said, and the old man snorted.

Davy took his men to the west side of the road, not confident they would not be shot at, although the fight had gone southward until there was no longer any gunfire. It was still dark and now it was getting chilly as well.

Scouting was done Indian fashion. No man showed himself except when he passed from tree to tree. In darkness this was difficult to discern.

Davy heard the wagons moving, and gauged his southward progress to their sound in order to be in a position to locate ambushers before the wagons came into sight.

One of his men squawked as he nearly stumbled over a corpse. The man nearest to him was a soldier. He stopped to take the dead man's tomahawk and sheath knife. Someone else had taken his rifle.

They found Davy's horse and beyond it, where the Choctaws had palavered, a dead Indian. Again, someone had already gleaned his rifle, but no one had taken his hatchet or knife.

Davy's companions proved to be fair stalkers. He thought this arose from the fact that they were green at this kind of scouting and fearful. A little fear under these circumstances was a good thing.

Davy was sashaying from the roadway back into the forest. His companions followed this example. One of them was moving toward the road when an Indian dropped on him from a tree. The wagoner did not have time to cry out. He only had time to bend low and buck like a horse. Even though the Indian was flung off, his slashing knife cut half the ear off the scout. Few parts of the body bleed as copiously as an ear.

The scout tried to bring his rifle to bear, but the Indian was as lithe as a panther. He caught the barrel in both hands and wrenched as hard as he could. Now, finally, the scout yelled.

The Indian swung the rifle like a club, knocked the scout down, and dropped the gun to lunge with his knife when a gunshot dropped him almost atop the scrambling man with the bloody ear.

128

Davy appeared, saw the bloody shirt of the wagoner, and told him to go find the wagons and get patched up.

The man who had shot the Indian moved out of shadows, jaws slowly moving, considered his victim, spat aside, and, without looking at Davy, faded back into the gloom to continue scouting.

For a mile neither band of scouts had encounters. On the east side they had not even come across dead men. On the west side Davy was scouting ahead when he came across a wounded Choctaw. The man was sitting propped against a tree, his rifle lying nearby. When he saw Davy, he remained expressionless. They exchanged a long look before Davy kicked the rifle out of the man's reach and left him. A few minutes later a swamper came up, asked if Davy had seen the wounded Indian, got a nod for a reply, then said: "You should've shot him."

Davy answered matter-of-factly: "There are more somewhere southward or around. If I'd shot him, they would have heard it." He eyed the swamper, who was young. "Did you look at him?"

"Yes."

"Then there's something you may have noticed. When he blinked his eyes, he did it real slow."

"I didn't pay him that much heed."

"Animals that know they're going to die do that. Next time you wound something, watch its eyes."

He left the swamper looking after him, came to a clearing where horses had cropped the feed right down to the ground, and leaned on his rifle, looking out into the clearing. He could clearly hear the wagons.

If there had been ambushers, they should have at least attempted to shoot the team horses by now.

He angled toward the road. The wagons were moving without haste. Southward the forest thinned out on both sides of the road.

He was turning back into the trees to find his companions when a flurry of gunfire erupted southward. Not close, but not far either.

He went searching for his companions, who had also heard the gunfire and were seeking Davy. Where they came together, one of the swampers said they'd better halt the wagons. That had sounded like a big band of riflemen down yonder. Davy did not agree that the wagons should be stopped. When he turned back to find the wagons, the men followed in his tracks like hunting dogs.

Dawn had come and passed. Humidity was high and the sky had a thin, unbroken overcast from horizon to horizon. That powder-horn moon had been right; it was going to rain.

Davy stayed within hearing distance of the road without going close enough to it to have a sighting. Whoever had been involved in that southerly gunfight would either be coming back after scattering whoever they'd been shooting at, or coming together farther down the road to attack when the wagons appeared.

He did not speculate about the fierce, brief exchange of gunfire beyond the location. His primary concern as he went northward was finding the wagons.

130

The forest's gloom had brightened slightly. It would not get much brighter but visibility was fair when a man's eyes were accustomed to the gloom.

Davy found a saddled horse, reins dragging as it browsed along. He did not approach it, but from that spot on he watched the area with heightened interest.

He did not find the man who owned the horse, which did not have to be significant; a free animal would graze and browse for a considerable distance.

He hadn't passed the horse by more than a few yards when he saw a slouched man sitting on a log. At his feet was a rifle with a shattered stock. He thought the man had been wounded and watched him from shadows for a long time. He was whittling a green twig with his sheath knife. Davy got the impression the man was totally detached from his surroundings and his peril.

Davy approached the man from the rear. If the whittler heard him, he gave no sign of it. He sat slouched and whittling right up until Davy spoke to him.

"You been hurt, mister?"

The man acted as though he had heard nothing; long green slivers of soft wood continued to peel off the twig.

Davy tried again. "There's a horse back yonder. If it's yours, I'll fetch it."

The slouched man continued to whittle. Davy briefly wondered if he was deaf. He stepped over the log and sat down. The man continued to whittle. Davy leaned his rifle aside. The man finally stopped whittling.

131

Without looking around or speaking, he pointed with his knife.

About thirty feet ahead, partially covered with leaves, was a face-down body with an arrow shaft protruding from the back up high. The stranger went back to whittling. Davy went to the body, leaned to lift it until he could see the face, before easing it back down.

The man said — "My boy." — and raised a weathered face with tears on both cheeks. "My only boy. I told him to stay back, but he come anyway." The man went back to whittling.

Davy left the man, coursing ahead until he reached an area where a dead horse was lying. From here on there were signs of a fierce fight, broken tree limbs, trampled undergrowth, churned earth, and the lingering scent of burned powder.

He scouted about a mile below this place, angled in the direction of the road, and sat down.

The wagons were coming. There were a few birds. He decided to go back to where the whittler had been sitting. The man was gone, so was the lad with the arrow in his back. Farther back he found where the lost horse had been caught, loaded, and was being led westerly.

When the wagons arrived, Davy was sitting on the verge. Cain was driving the first wagon, which meant his party of scouts had found nothing on the east side and had returned to the wagons.

He dusted off, went down where the lieutenant was astride a gaunt horse, and leaned on his rifle. The officer raised his uninjured arm for the cavalcade to halt.

Davy said: "No ambushers for another mile. Beyond there, it looks like open country."

The lieutenant straightened in his saddle, looked both east and west, told Davy there was an extra horse at the tailgate of the last wagon, and made his arm gesture for the wagons to begin moving. His command was united again.

Davy got astride the extra horse — which was the mount of the bugler — and waited for the forest to yield to somewhat rolling, mostly treeless country.

When they halted at a full-fledged stream with a bridge over it to water the animals and rest briefly in an area where they could see for miles in three directions, Cain came back where Davy was re-bridling after tanking up the bugler's horse and said: "Wasn't nary a soul where we scouted easterly." The old man put a shrewd gaze on Davy. "But you knowed there wouldn't be, didn't you."

Davy accepted Cain's offer of Kentucky twist, returned the plug, and said: "I can't figure out who won that fight or where they are. My guess is that Red Sash's band whupped the Choctaws an' run 'em off."

"Likely," the old man agreed.

"Then where is Red Sash?"

Cain scratched the tip of his nose before speaking. "All's I care about, Mister Crockett, is reachin' our destination, gettin' rid of this Army freight, findin' me a nice tavern with clean hay in the loft, an' you can have everythin' else."

Davy did not mention the whittler. It would serve no purpose and their meeting had seemed to be one of those things that had no place in casual conversation.

They left the creek ground over the bridge, and had a settlement in view when Davy decided he would cut loose and head for home.

Up ahead old Cain let out a howl that caught everyone's attention. Several hundred yards onward where clay hills lay on both sides of the road and ran southward for some distance, there was a band of horsemen blocking the road as motionless as stone carvings.

The lieutenant sent for Davy and asked if he recognized any of the men barring the road. The distance was too great so Davy volunteered to ride ahead for a closer look.

Actually this had been the reason the lieutenant had sent for Davy. He offered a pistol and an admonition. "Don't get so close they can hold you hostage."

Davy ignored both the pistol and the admonition. Around the officer his soldiers sat in silence, watching Davy ride ahead. One of the soldiers, a grizzled man, said: "If that's Breaux, all's I got to say is he don't give up."

The lieutenant's reply was curt. "We're too close to a settlement for renegades to make trouble."

Whether that was true or not, none of the watchers spoke as Davy got closer to the motionless blockaders.

Davy abruptly drew rein, shifted Betsy to his left arm, and raised his right hand palm forward as he called out. "Jesse!"

One of the riders urged his horse ahead. Where they met some distance from the blockading riders, Jesse Jones smiled. "There was talk in the settlement about a big fight up yonder. Last night some Indians come through . . . went wide around the settlement. I was goin' to go south where the boy's folks was massacred, but the other fellers thought we'd best go north an' find them Army wagons. Was you in that fight, Davy?"

"I was part of it." Davy looked past at the horsemen barring the road. "Is there a reason they don't figure to let us pass?"

"No reason at all. What we figured was that so many fellers comin' with the wagons bein' led with a feller in buckskin out front, it might be the fight was over the wagons an' the Army lost. Davy, it's a blessin' to see you again."

"It's a blessing to be here, Jesse. How's Bess an' the children?"

"Fat 'n' sassy. Davy, you recollect the lad named Knight whose folks them raiders killed?"

"How is he, Jesse?"

"He's back yonder with the others. His first name's Reno. Most likely this ain't the place for it, but I'd like to ask you a question."

"Go ahead."

"I been takin' the boy with me. I been takin' him around with me. He's a good lad. Davy, I'd be right grateful if you'd let me 'n' the lad build a cabin on the west side of your clearing."

Davy's mind flashed back to another youngster — with an arrow in his back. Jesse thought Davy's hesitation meant something else. He said: "I know it'd make a crowd, us an' you 'uns, but to be right honest with you, Davy, I had no young 'uns and the lad needs someone."

Davy leaned, slapped the older man lightly on the shoulder as he said: "Let me get shed of these soldiers an' their wagons, then you 'n' me, the lad an' maybe some of my boys can help build the cabin. Jesse? Can you get them men to quit barring the road?"

Jesse smiled and started to rein around. "We just didn't know is all, what with all the talk of a big fight. I'll take 'em back to the settlement."

Davy rode at a walk back where the lieutenant and the others were waiting. He swung his horse and without a word joined the men around him in watching the riders heading southward toward the settlement.

The officer said: "What happened, Mister Crockett? Who were they?"

"That feller I talked to is a partner of mine. He rounded up them fellers to hunt Choctaws for killing an' burning." Davy raised his rein hand, which was a signal for the teamsters to get their hitches moving. The officer rode through the narrow place in the road with Davy. Once he stood in his stirrups and said: "How big's that settlement?"

"Couple hundred, I'd guess. Big enough so's no one'll attack it while you 'n' your men rest up. There ain't no doctor there, but there's a real handy midwife." Davy slouched in the saddle. He had missed a lot of sleep and some meals. His arm ached where he'd been unable to avoid a knife, but he was no more than half a day's ride from Bess, their clutch of nestlings, and a place to set down and let loose.

The lieutenant roused Davy from his thoughts. "I got authority to pay a scout for the rest of the trip, Mister Crockett."

Davy did not even look at the man, riding stirrup with him. "Mister, there ain't enough money in the whole danged country to keep me from going home."

The lieutenant was understanding, but he was also pig-stubborn. "When my report gets read by senior officers, if you're of a mind, I'd like to get them to offer you an Army commission. The pay's better'n grubbin' the ground, the Army supplies horses an' uniforms, it even pays for your food and bed."

Davy finally turned toward the lieutenant. "That's right decent of you, Lieutenant, but I've soldiered my share as a volunteer, and to speak right out, I'll say, if the choice was between skinning skunks an' being an Army officer, I'd take skinning skunks."

The lieutenant reddened and rode without another word until they could make out every detail of the settlement, then he asked its name. Davy answered candidly: "I can't rightly say, but when I left, it was called Shoal Crossing."

"Why would it be changed?" the officer asked.

"Because settlements in this country change their names oftener'n I change my britches. Sooner or later they name themselves after presidents. Shoal Crossing might be Jacksonville by now, for all I know."

The one rutted wide roadway of the settlement was crowded with onlookers on both sides as the wagons entered from the north. People waved hats and smiled. The lieutenant took this homage to heart by removing his hat and bowing from the saddle until the people began shouting Davy's name, then the officer put his hat back on, and rode toward the corrals at the southern end of town as red as a beet.

CHAPTER
TWELVE

Colonel Crockett

Davy and Jesse slipped away, heading for the Crockett clearing, but in Shoal Crossing those volunteers Jesse had rounded up were not amenable to disbanding. After supper that evening they congregated at the tavern where the soldiers, muddy, bedraggled, but properly fed and red-faced, not altogether from the hearth fire, bought a round after which an old man with unkempt hair got on a chair, yelled for silence, and put forth an idea that had been discussed at supper.

"We got as good a party of fightin' men as is around!" he exclaimed. "Trouble in our territory ain't over with by a long shot. I say we form up a Shoal Crossing militia unit. If we just go on home, we'll get caught out sure as hell's hot the next time raiders come. I don't want that an' neither do you. I say we take turns havin' scouts out, organize ourselves so's we can't be caught alone from now on, and do things proper."

A sweaty, large-nosed man called from the bar. "I'm favorable, but we got to have a commander, like the Army does!"

The old man smiled so wide his few teeth showed. "Davy Crockett!" he exclaimed.

There was a hush as men looked around nodding. The lieutenant, warm inside and out, spoke from a table among his soldiers: "Captain Crockett!"

The old man seemed to ponder that briefly, then said: "*Colonel* Crockett."

The lieutenant emptied a tankard, and one of the enlisted men took it to the bar to be refilled. The lieutenant discreetly belched before smiling slyly. "Colonel for a fact. Maybe even General Crockett."

The old man scowled. "This ain't no joke, mister."

From the bar the red-nosed, sweaty man raised his tankard. "Colonel Davy Crockett, head Indian of the Shoal Crossing Militia!"

The enlisted soldier returned, placed the tankard before his officer, and leaned to say: "They like colonel, sir, an' there's some among them that's tanked up enough to fight."

It was good advice and the lieutenant accepted it. His injured arm was throbbing. He was as full as a tick and sweaty from liquor. He asked a villager where he could find the midwife.

The villager's initial reaction was a round-eyed stare. The officer touched his injured arm and the villager arose. "I'll take you to her cabin. She's already got your bugler tucked in."

The matter of organizing the Shoal Crossing Militia required half the night. The tavernkeeper was appointed quartermaster with the obligation to make sure, when the militia marched, he'd have the appropriate medicine in his wagon.

There were other appointments. The old man with unkempt hair, although proposed for several ranks, declined each time. He said he had no idea how to conduct himself except as a volunteer, in which capacity he had served during the Creek War and even down at New Orleans.

By the time the meeting at the tavern ended, miles northwesterly, Davy was asleep in a chair with Bess rocking gently as she mended the knife cut in his shirt.

Across the clearing an owl hooted. Bess sewed, rocked occasionally, looked at Davy, and softly shook her head. He needed an all-over bath at the creek; his whiskers scratched and he'd lost weight. What he'd told her before going to sleep in the chair was more than he'd told others.

His story of the man sitting whittling on a log with the body of his dead son close by touched Bess Crockett the way it would not have touched most men.

She had fed him, shooed the children to their loft, had mulled some cider for Davy, and had told him something about Reno Knight.

When Jesse had told the boy he and Davy had buried the lad's folks, Reno had fled from the house, had disappeared into the westerly forest, and, when he hadn't returned, Jesse had gone to find him.

She said she had no idea what Jesse had said, but when they returned together, although the boy hadn't eaten and shrank from the light, when he and Jesse had gone out to the porch, Bess thought the boy had got over the shock. She said she had no idea how Jesse had

141

done it, but beginning the day after Jesse brought the lad back from the forest, they became inseparable.

When Davy awakened along toward first light, Bess had finished with the shirt, had scrubbed it, and had it lying a fair distance from the fire to dry; too close the buckskin would stiffen and crack, too far and it wouldn't dry for days.

She told him to go to the creek and handed him a chunk of tan lye soap. After he'd departed, she gave his britches the same scrubbing and set them also to dry.

When Davy returned, she had his second pair of buckskins ready. By that time the children had been fed. They swarmed over Davy, sounding like a nest of trilling song birds.

John Wesley told his father that Reno had asked him to help stake out where a cabin was to be built. John Wesley took his hatchet and left the cabin.

Davy stood in the doorway. Across the clearing Jesse and the Knight lad had cut saplings to be sharpened to stakes and were awaiting John Wesley's arrival.

Bess came to the door. Davy explained what they were doing over yonder, told her of Jesse's question, and Davy's answer.

Bess smiled. "He's a good man, Davy. The children are right fond of him."

Davy looked down at his wife. Over the years he had made a discovery. Bess Crockett saw good in everyone, which was unusual in a frontier country where trust was fine but only when folks were facing one another. Turning one's back to a stranger, even to some acquaintances, had resulted in wooden crosses in some isolated places.

Davy was over tying twine between stakes when someone he had not expected to see again came riding across the clearing. As the lieutenant dismounted, Davy noticed the clean bandage showing past the tunic where the officer carried his injured arm.

The lieutenant nodded to Jesse and the two boys before addressing Davy as Colonel Crockett. Jesse, the boys, and Davy stood like stone. The lieutenant told Davy about the formation of the Shoal Crossing Militia, that Davy had been elected colonel commander, and held out his hand. "Congratulations, Colonel. If more settlements would organize militias, the Army's job would be easier. I've got to get back. We're going on south to deliver the freight. If I'm ever down this way again, I'd admire to call on you, Colonel."

The lieutenant smiled, something Davy had never seen him do before. He gripped the extended hand and smiled back. He held the horse's bit as the officer mounted, released it, and stepped back. "I'd feel better about you going iffen I knew where them renegades are, Lieutenant."

"I hired some of your militia to ride escort an' scout for the rest of the trip," the officer said, nodded to Davy, to Jesse and the boys, reined around, and loped back the way he had come.

Jesse spat amber, considered the hatchet he'd been using to pound stakes, and dryly said: "I always figured you was set for better things in life." Then he laughed.

John Wesley and Reno Knight were impressed. Reno in particular showed diffidence until Davy caught hold of him, swung Reno athwart his shoulders, and said: "Let's get something to eat. I'm hungrier'n a bear cub."

At the cabin the boys told Bess why the soldier had ridden to the clearing. She evinced less diffidence as she got them all seated to be fed and said: "Colonel . . . sir . . . you went an' left the soap at the creek. The girls fetched it back. It's a chore making soap. I'd take it kindly if you wouldn't forget to fetch it back . . . Colonel."

It was a noisy meal. It could not have been otherwise with nine children. Bess and one of the older girls kept food coming.

Davy heard a dog bark above the noise in the cabin and paid no attention until Jesse looked up from his platter with his head cocked as he said: "Now who's comin'?"

Two boys went to look from the doorway, returned, and said they had seen no one.

The dogs continued to bark. Davy listened to one particular dog, old Ned, his favorite bear dog. He leaned to arise. Across from him Jesse stood up, saying: "Darned varmints, country's gettin' full of 'em." He went to the doorway, stepped outside under the overhang, and squinted across the clearing in which direction the dogs were snarling.

The gunshot was loud because the man who fired was close to the final fringe of trees.

Everyone inside heard the shot and also heard something strike the cabin's outside wall. Davy was on his feet in seconds.

144

Jesse was lying on one side with an outflung arm. His blood darkened where hard ground absorbed it. With Bess helping, they got Jesse inside, placed him flat out near the fireplace atop a bearskin rug, and Davy knelt to cut the shirt where blood ran. Bess told one of the girls to get a basin of hot water from the stove; she told another girl to get the children into the loft where they were to be quiet.

She elbowed Davy aside, rolled up her sleeves, and, when the water arrived, she told the girl who had brought it to fetch the herb box and her sewing kit. She faced her husband over the inert figure on the rug. "Mind the boy," she said.

Reno was near the open door, reaching for Jesse's rifle when Davy approached, took the weapon from the lad, and leaned it aside as the boy looked up with wet eyes. "I got to do it, Mister Crockett. I got to do it. First my dog, then my folks . . . Seems everything I love gets killed. He's going to die, ain't he?"

Davy leaned down with a hand on Reno's shoulder. "If I know Jesse Jones, I'd say he's been shot worse an' never stopped talking."

"He's yonder in them trees, Mister Crockett."

"Son, by now he's a mile off an' still going."

"I want him, Mister Crockett."

Davy was about to speak when Jesse groaned. The lad crossed the room in long strides, sank to both knees with tears streaming. Jesse turned his head slightly and smiled, something he was not much given to doing. "I'm goin' to need some waitin' on, Reno."

Bess straightened up, her back ached. Her arms were bloody to the elbow. She used the back of one hand to brush hair away, and, when Davy came up, she dropped something into his hand as she said: "It's not lead, Davy. It's not heavy enough."

Davy took the ball to better light and examined it. Steel musket balls were genuine novelties on the frontier where men used molds into which they poured molten lead to make ammunition. Farther north, where they had factories to manufacture such things by the hundreds, steel musket balls were common.

He pocketed the steel ball, went over, and sank to one knee as Bess spoke to Jesse. "If he was aiming for your brisket, he was too far to the left. Your side looks like a butchered hawg. Take a deep breath."

Jesse obeyed and gasped.

Bess leaned forward, feeling for broken ribs. She found two and asked one of the girls for the whiskey jug. She then explained to Jesse that with two broken ribs and maybe another cracked one, he'd be doing good if he could whittle a stick for two or three months.

Jesse said nothing until he'd had two long pulls from the jug and let Davy take it, then he made a ghastly smile at Bess as he spoke in a harsh whisper. "I've got to be up 'n' around long before then, ma'am. I got to hang some ambushin' damned rascal's hair out to dry."

They made a pallet for Jesse atop the bear robe, stoked up the fire, sat with him until his eyes closed, then Davy took his wife aside. She anticipated his question. "He's not young, but it ain't the busted bones. They'll heal. He's lost a sight of blood."

146

Davy listened, nodded, glanced over his wife's head to the open doorway, kissed her forehead, got his rifle from beside the door, and slipped swiftly outside to the south side of the cabin, waited until he heard birds in the westerly woods, then ran across cleared ground and disappeared into the forest.

The gunshot had come from the west not the east. It required a lot of time for Davy to make a wide sashay northward through thick timber before he could start southward. By the time he found where the ambusher had knelt, the sun was slanting away.

There had been six of them. One wore boots; the other five wore moccasins. He had no difficulty locating the area where their horses had been tethered, or of the direction in which the animals had been ridden after the shooting — northward for more than a mile, then on an angle in the direction of the distant road.

Tracking an area where gloom was perpetual was not easy, but Davy had an advantage. He was on foot. As the gloom deepened along toward day's end, he was less than a mile from the same road where the wagon fight had occurred. He had been able to make good time right up until sundown. After that he had to slacken considerably in order to detect disturbed leaves, an occasional trampled small bush, and limbs that had been broken where riders had pushed past.

He had his powder horn and bullet pouch slung from each shoulder, but he had not taken his parfleche. That meant he would have to go hungry. It did not bother him even after he found where the ambushers had left the forest for the road.

Here, while the light was marginally better, the tracking was hindered by dozens of sets of horse tracks, some going north, some going south.

He had to proceed a few feet at a time with dark forests on each side of the road and the silence that ordinarily accompanied nightfall, when he heard two gunshots.

He left the road, hid in the westerly forest, and waited. Northward some distance there was the sound of horses moving swiftly from the road to the forest. It sounded as though riders were scattering among the trees.

The silence deepened and was not disturbed for a long time before Davy picked up a familiar scent — wood smoke. That was not extraordinary in a country where to save candles folks bedded down early. He was not surprised. Hearth fires could put smoke up a chimney for a long time, often until the coals were rekindled the following morning.

What baffled him was not just the scent but those two gunshots and the discovery of riders in this area that was not very far south from where the wagon fight had taken place. When he had previously scouted this area, he had not seen a clearing.

He moved cautiously seeking the cleared ground that commonly accompanied a house. Those two gunshots had not come from somewhere this far north, but from easterly toward the roadway.

He did not find the clearing for an excellent reason; there was none. What he found was a house made of unusually large logs nestled among a stand of big trees.

What held his attention longest was one scraped rawhide window showing light from within.

He hesitated in forest darkness. Once before he had come upon a place like this. That time the reason there had been no clearing was that the settler did not farm, he trapped.

It was not possible from a distance to make out much except that the house had been built like a fort and the roof hadn't been shingled with sugar-pine slabs; it was covered with sod. If there was a stock pen, he could not make it out. In any case it would have been behind the house.

The only way to approach the house was to one side of it where the trees were as thick as the hair on a dog's back. It would take time.

Someone appeared in the cabin doorway and flung away a basin of water. For a fact no one washed clothes or bathed after dark.

He began working his way toward the house, was close enough to make out someone moving back and forth through the hide window without being able to distinguish anything except that it was a person, when a dog barked. A big dog. Davy heard it hit the end of a chain. He'd heard frightened horses hit the end of a chain that hard but never a dog.

The rawhide window went dark. The snarling dog lunged several more times as Davy moved a yard at a time in the direction of the animal. Its lunging and snarling increased.

When he finally could see it lunge and rear, he stopped dead still. It wasn't a dog; it was a wolf, the largest one he had ever seen. He knew what it was, but buffalo wolves hadn't been seen in his country since the last buffalo herds had been so diminished that the remnants migrated west. Many miles west.

He moved back into the forest, changed course to sidle around behind the house. The big wolf no longer lunged on its chain but its snarling did not stop.

There was a large animal pen behind the cabin made of smaller logs. In it were two big mules. They had caught his scent and were standing shoulder-to-shoulder, marking his progress by man smell.

There was a lean-to built on the back of the house made of smaller logs. Davy was familiar with the smell of the lean-to before he got to the corral. The lean-to was a smokehouse.

He stood beside a huge old tree and with eyes accustomed to darkness waited and watched. If the man inside shoved a rifle barrel through a gun hole, Davy would hear it, but nothing like that happened. Eventually even the wolf got quiet.

Men like Davy Crockett developed powerful instincts. What instinct told him now was that no one would build a fort-like cabin deep in a forest where killers of all kinds and colors hunted without growing an eye in the back of his head and building a cabin that could not be burned or blown apart.

Whoever was in the cabin had been warned by the wolf and had put out his candles. This left whatever adversary was outside with the initiative while all the man inside had to do was wait.

150

Davy was considering a stalk when a quiet deep voice spoke from somewhere near the rear of the house. "Fish or cut bait. You can't burn me out. You can't knock down the walls. If you move, I'll put you down with a broken back for the rest of your life."

The voice had been deep and rumbling, which meant the man was big. It hadn't sounded worried. Davy almost smiled. Whoever he was, he'd been tested before. Davy hung the rifle in the crook of his arm and called back: "My name's Crockett! I got no bone to pick with you."

For a moment there was silence, then the large man said: "Step out where I can see you *if* you're Davy Crockett."

The wolf had stopped snarling at the sound of its owner's voice. Davy moved clear of the large tree, walked toward the side of the mule pen, halted, and waited. The other man said: "A mite closer."

Davy went down the side of the pen until the other man said: "I'll be blessed! I seen you with Jackson's Army some time back. You was with another feller, older'n you. Come ahead."

The man was large, almost big enough to hand-wrestle a bear. He had a gray beard and a mop of bushy hair that likely hadn't seen soap or a comb in months.

When they shook hands, the older man's fist engulfed Davy's hand. He led the way to the lean-to, from there through a slab door inside the main cabin, but he stopped before opening the door to say: "I got two hurt fellers inside. Come blunderin' along like drunks. My dog helped me find 'em."

Inside, the bear of a man went around lighting candles. He pointed to a pair of pallets. "One of 'em's not goin' to make it." He pointed to one of the bundles near his fireplace but what caught and held Davy's attention was an elegant beaver hat that looked worse than the last time he had seen it.

The large man said: "Most of the time he's out of his head. Look at them boots 'n' that hat. He ain't one of us for a fact."

The second pallet held another motionless figure, buried under robes. The big man said: "I knew that 'un years back. He sold guns an' powder to the Creeks. His name's Ezra Baldridge. By the way, I'm Carl Mitchell. Baldridge ain't hurt bad but the other one . . ." Mitchell wagged his head. "I couldn't make out his name."

Davy leaned Betsy aside, crossed to Beaver Hat, and studied the sweaty face of the man on the pallet. It was the man he had eavesdropped on before the wagon fight.

The large man came over, leaned, squinted, and said: "He won't make it till dawn."

Davy asked if the large man had whiskey. Mitchell nodded. "I got whiskey. I make it out back in decent weather."

"Let's pour some down . . . what'd you say his name was?"

"I couldn't make it out."

From the second pallet Ezra Baldridge said: "Name I know him by is Mason. He's some sort of trader. I been with him some months. Guide sort of."

Mitchell brought the jug. While Davy held up the man's head, Mitchell poured whiskey until the wounded man had to swallow.

Davy went to the other wounded man. When their eyes met, Davy said: "You 'n' another feller was with Beaver Hat when you met Charley Ben's renegades."

The injured man's eyes widened. "You wasn't there. Who are you?"

Mitchell boomed the answer. "He's Davy Crockett. You never heard of Davy Crockett?"

The gray-faced man under robes on the floor weakly nodded. "Yup, I've heard of Crockett, but you wasn't around when we met them Indians."

"I was there," Davy stated. "Back in the forest. I heard what Mason told the Indians about little hand bombs. What I'd like to know is how you 'n' Mason knew how to meet the Creeks."

"Mason got an Indian to find a good meetin' place. He found a big white rock. Indians set store by such things. When the Indian come back, he sent me to find the Choctaws an' set up a meetin' at the white rock."

Davy hoisted the jug, swallowed twice, handed it back to the large man who also swallowed twice, then put the jug on a handmade table with one leg shorter than the others, which tipped from the jug's weight.

Davy moved back to Beaver Hat, who was sweating. His face was red and his eyes were brightly fixed on Davy. He had heard what his companion had said, and spoke in an almost normal tone of voice.

"Mister Mitchell told me he's never seen a man walk away who's been shot through like I've been."

The large man solemnly nodded his head as he regarded the man called Mason. "I can't figure how you got this far."

Mason ignored the large man. "Davy Crockett," he said almost pensively. "Where I met Charley Ben they had scouts out."

Davy nodded. "Did you count 'em when they came back?"

Mason's thin lips quirked. "One shy, but Indians come an' go like autumn leaves. Mister Mitchell, another pull on the jug?"

Davy shook his head. "You figured you'd shot me," he said, making it more of a statement than a question.

Mason's answer was crisp. "If you'd got shot, you wouldn't be standin' there, would you?"

Davy had another question. "What happened to you and your friend?"

"When we reached the road, the Indians didn't want to leave the forest an' they didn't want to go north, so me 'n' Ezra started out alone. They shot us from behind, took our guns and horses, and rode back into the forest." Mason made a mirthless smile. "They were mad that another band of renegades was already waiting for the wagons. Charley Ben accused me of double-crossing him. He lost warriors in the wagon fight. I was glad to get shed of him." Mason's face was losing color as he muttered. "I had no idea others were after those wagons."

CHAPTER
THIRTEEN

Siege!

Davy emptied both shot pouches of the wounded men; each pouch contained steel musket balls. Because Mason had lapsed into a stupor, Davy knelt beside Baldridge's pallet, holding two steel balls in his hand. As he did this, he said: "There was you 'n' Mason an' another man at the meeting with Charley Ben's raiders. Where is he an' what's his name?"

Mitchell let the wounded man have a sip of whiskey before Davy got his answer. "That'd be Moses Owens. Him 'n' me was together better'n two years."

"Where is he now?" Davy asked.

"I got no idea, but I think he rode off with the Indians after that scrap with the soldiers at the wagons." The wounded man ran a dry tongue over parched lips. Mitchell interpreted this correctly and shook his head. "You had enough."

Davy looked over where Mason was feebly moving under his blankets. Mitchell said: "Won't be long. He bled like a stuck hawg."

Davy returned to Mason's pallet, but the man's eyes did not focus; his face was gray and, although his lips moved, no sound came out. Mitchell stepped past, knelt to feel Mason's neck, and stood up as he said one word: "Gone."

He had been right; it wasn't quite dawn, but it was close enough.

Mitchell put food on his rickety table. Davy ate, drank spring water, and listened to Mitchell give the details of how he had found the wounded men.

He eventually returned to the pallet of the remaining gunshot man to ask where Baldridge had got those steel musket balls. The answer offered no surprise. "From Mason. Him 'n' Owens met me north of Shoal Creek. They had a pack horse with them steel slugs on it. He give us both a couple handfuls. He said they shot truer'n lead slugs, an' for a fact they do."

"Where were you 'n' Mason going up north?"

"I don't rightly know where. He told me there'd be a town up yonder. He was mad that Owens didn't come with us."

"Owens left you 'n' him after the wagon fight?"

"Yes, I already told you that. I figured the Red Sticks killed him or he went over to them."

The wolf growled. Mitchell went around, blowing out candles. In an almost off-hand way he said — "This place is gettin' right popular." — and disappeared through his lean-to door, musket in hand.

Davy sat in darkness, listening to the snarling animal. It was not raising the kind of ruckus it had raised when he had approached. This time the snarling was more like a growl.

Baldridge spoke softly in darkness. "Indians. They're all around, bands of 'em killing anything that moves. They'll kill us."

Davy said nothing. He went to the hide window, not to peer out but to listen. The wolf's growls were diminishing.

Mitchell returned without a sound, unusual for a man his size and heft. He leaned the rifle aside and spoke quietly: "Nothin' as far as I could figure. My dawg'll sound like that sometimes when varmints are passin' along."

He would have relit the candles but Davy thought it wouldn't hurt to wait a bit. Mitchell shrugged in silence.

In darkness the wounded man said: "They sneak up on you like ghosts. They're out there, sure as I'm lying here."

Davy returned to Baldridge's pallet to ask a question. "Which one of you tried to shoot me?"

Baldridge tipped his head as far back as it would go and said: "It was him. He'd seen you with the wagons. I expect he knew who you were. Anyway, after the fight he took me 'n' some of them Choctaws to your clearing."

"How'd he know where it was?" Davy asked.

Baldridge feebly shook his head. "I've got no idea, but he knew. The Indians didn't like crouching in the trees. They were going to leave when Mason offered them some gold money." Baldridge nodded in the direction of a pair of saddlebags. "In a pouch on the left side."

"Did you see Mason shoot?"

"I was behind him when we thought it was you stepped outside. I'd have got you plumb center. Who was that feller he shot?"

Mitchell was at the table with Mason's saddlebags, pawing inside like a bear at a honey tree. He found the doeskin pouch and held it aloft, grinning from ear to ear. He asked Baldridge why the Indians hadn't taken the pouch. The answer was peevish. "They didn't know he had it. Money doesn't mean much to Indians anyway. I knew he had money. I'd seen the pouch when he gave some to the Choctaws at the Crockett place. I never knew how much . . . *listen!*"

The wolf was growling. Even in daylight it was a sound to make the hair stand up; in darkness the sound was capable of making blood run cold in brave men.

Davy edged up to the window. There was a steely tint to the sky. Dawn was coming. The wolf's growl became deeper, more like a snarl.

Mitchell dropped the doeskin pouch and stood like a statue. "It's somethin' more'n passin' varmints," he said quietly.

Baldridge struggled to rise up on his pallet. "Indians! I can feel 'em."

Davy got his rifle and returned to the scraped-hide window. If Baldridge was right, if indeed it was Indians, were they men who had been near his clearing when Mason had shot Jesse, or was it some of Red Sash's renegades on a prowl?

The bear of a man quietly said: "There's more'n one out there."

158

Davy leaned beside the window, watching the sky brighten. There was another possibility; perhaps both bands of renegades, at least some of both bands, were out there. Renegades were notorious for changing sides. Whoever they were, they wouldn't wait until full daylight, and, when they brought the fight to the cabin, there would be only Mitchell and Davy to fight them off. The cabin was like a fort, which was an advantage, but if there were very many attackers . . .

Davy jerked straight up when the gun went off, not outside, but inside the house. He spun in time to see the big man withdrawing his rifle from a loophole in the wall. Mitchell said: "That'll teach the varmint to try 'n' knife my dog."

From the pallet Baldridge said: "Indian?"

Mitchell looked around without answering. He went to work recharging his rifle. As he did this, he addressed Davy. "White feller in buckskin. Who'd that be?"

Davy's answer was brief. "Charley Ben's renegades were Choctaws with some Creeks among 'em."

"That warn't no tomahawk, Davy."

"Red Sash, Mister Mitchell."

"Who'n hell is Red Sash?" Mitchell asked, leaning his reloaded rifle aside.

Baldridge was struggling to get clear of his robes. Mitchell turned on him. "Lie down, you fool. You'll start that arm to bleedin' again."

Baldridge seemed deaf. He looked at Davy. "Help me up."

159

Mitchell crossed to the pallet, put a ham-sized hand on Baldridge, and forced him back down. Baldridge protested. "It's not my rifle arm. Just the two of you can't . . ."

"Lie still!" the large man exclaimed, increasing the pressure on Baldridge's chest.

"I can help! Let me up!"

"All you'll do," growled the large man, "is get in the way. Now lie still or I'll crack your skull. *Lie still!*"

Where Davy was standing to one side of the window, an arrow came through, tore the scraped hide, crossed the room, and embedded itself in the far wall. Mitchell was regarding the arrow shaft when he dryly said: "Mister Red Sash don't just have whites, does he?"

Davy did not answer. Through the tear in the window's hide he could see trees, underbrush, and a man lying face down just out of reach of the chained wolf. Otherwise he could see no one, or any movement.

It would be a while before the sun climbed high enough to shed light above the trees. Even then, as dense as the woodland was, sunshine would be spotty.

The big man crossed to the door leading to his smokehouse, disappeared, and Davy heard steel sliding over wood as Mitchell used a gun hole.

Davy braced for the gunshot, but there was none. Baldridge distracted him by saying: "I can shoot. It's my left shoulder that got hurt."

Davy considered the gray face in poor light. Baldridge was frightened enough to ignore pain and bleeding. Davy took the jug to him, waited until the wounded man had swallowed three times, then returned the jug to the table, all without a word.

Baldridge subsided but not quickly. When he did lie back, he was breathing loudly. It was the only sound until two gunshots, erupting almost simultaneously in the rear of the house, brought Davy to the smokehouse door.

The big man was standing to one side of his gun port, reloading. It was impossible to make out much in the small room with no windows. Mitchell said: "He was sneakin' along, bent over with a firebrand in his hand . . . the danged idiot. I could see him when he come out of the trees. Mister Crockett, maybe Red Sash is experienced, but that idiot warn't, tryin' to sneak up close, holdin' a lighted torch." Mitchell snorted, leaned to peek out his rifle hole, straightened back around, and sighed. "They can't burn us out."

Davy returned to the main room. Baldridge's breathing was loud, and now uneven. Davy looked down as he passed. Baldridge shouldn't have taken that last big pull from the jug. Or maybe he should have, because for a fact however the fight ended, he wouldn't know.

Someone fired a rifle on the south side of the cabin. There were no windows in the south wall. Davy went over and listened. Outside someone was hurriedly reloading. Another man spoke but Davy was unable to distinguish much except that the language was English.

Some distance from the cabin a man threw back his head and howled like a wolf. Mitchell's dog did not reply. Maybe the howl was good enough to fool men but it was not authentic enough to earn a reply from Mitchell's wolf.

Another gun fired, this one from around front. The slug tore more hide from the window and ricocheted, striking fireplace stone about where Baldridge lay passed out, inert.

Mitchell appeared soundlessly. "They're around the house," he told Davy. "They got to be figurin', because they ain't shootin' very much. Tell me, how seasoned is this Red Sash feller?"

That was an easy question to answer. "He fought with the British during the war. He's some kind of Frenchman from Canada. He's as seasoned as you'd expect."

Mitchell looked around at Baldridge. Davy said: "Passed out." Mitchell ran bent fingers through his mass of gray thatch. "I got a way outen here, but not until we got no choice."

Davy waited for more but Mitchell did not explain. Two guns fired on a slanting angle from the southeast corner of the cabin, where those renegades Davy had heard talking had been. One slug went wild but the second one came through the window and buried itself in the northern wall.

Mitchell was scornful. "They got to do better'n that."

Davy said: "They will. We're forted up, but they got all the time they'll need."

Mitchell sidled close to the window with the shattered hide, leaned carefully to look out, and someone opposite the cabin saw movement by the window and fired from the forest.

A sliver of wood gashed the big man's cheek. He got away from the window with one hand to his bleeding face. In the sickly light Davy said: "That's the one place you don't want to hover, Mister Mitchell. That's the only place they can see in. They'll have riflemen amongst them trees."

Mitchell held a blue cloth to his face. Acting as though he hadn't come within an ace of getting his head shot off, he said: "I'm hungry, Davy. You? I got some smoked bear meat an' wild turnips, an' I got coffee."

They moved the table clear of random bullets coming through the window and the big man fired up his corner hearth stove made of stone. While holding the bloody cloth to his face, he got a fire going, went to the lean-to for meat, returned, and, while passing the table, scooped up the jug, took a long pull, set it down, and returned to his cooking area. If two men were ideal for situations like this, it was Davy Crockett and Carl Mitchell. With killers around their log house and an occasional bullet coming through the window, they ate heartily. For the time being with poor but increasing visibility there was little else to be done and both men were hungry.

For a long time there was no gunfire, no sounds of any kind before the man who had howled like a wolf made the same call again.

This time Davy arose from the table, took Betsy to the south wall, and leaned to listen. When he faced Mitchell, he said: "Digging."

The big man arose, belched, and came to the wall also to listen. He straightened up, wagging his head. "They'll be all day gettin' under the fir logs set deep. Davy, we can make it hot for 'em."

They went to the dark smokehouse where Mitchell gently eased aside a greasy log that slid soundlessly. Mitchell said: "It's how I vent out smoke. If a man leans out, he can see along the south wall."

Davy did not lean. "There'll be watchers, Mister Mitchell."

The large man nodded agreement, twisted to lift a round small rough-wood cask from a shelf, and said: "When I pitch it out, you watch for 'em to run."

Davy raised Betsy. When the cask struck the ground, a startled man squawked, jumped up, and ran. Davy shot him but not badly enough for the man to fall. While Davy was reloading, Mitchell eased his rifle through the opening, tracked another fleeing individual, and fired. The fleeing man threw out both arms, dropped his rifle, and stumbled as far as a tree before collapsing.

Someone yelled and within moments guns fired in the direction of the opening in the smokehouse wall. Davy was flattened on one side; Mitchell was flattened on the other side.

This time the attack was concerted and fierce. Neither Davy nor the large man was able to leave their protective logs until Davy heard something and yelled

164

for Mitchell to follow as he ran into the main part of the cabin. Something struck the door with resounding force. Mitchell started for the window that would allow him to look northward where the door was. Davy shouted at him, and Mitchell stopped at the exact moment when riflemen in the opposite trees fired through the window.

The door was struck again. The force of the blow made the entire massive front wall quiver.

Mitchell called to Davy: "They'll bust it loose!"

He was right; the forged-iron hinges were loosening as the wood cracked.

In the midst of this peril Baldridge came out of his stupor, twisted as the door was struck a third time, saw the wood crack, and cried out.

Neither Davy nor Mitchell heeded Baldridge. They took positions on both sides of the shattering door with their rifles.

One length of slab-wood broke. Through the gap Davy saw the men using their log ram. He stepped around where he had good aim and fired. At the same time Mitchell gave a yell and also fired through the gap.

The log ram fell as its handlers fled. Two of them did not flee.

Now the only sound was Baldridge. Davy got the jug, told him to swallow four times, put the jug back on the rickety table, and went to the door to reload.

Mitchell said: "That ain't a natural way to fight. Indians'd never do somethin' like that."

Davy nodded as he said — "It ain't just Indians out there." — and risked a peek through the gap. He caught a fleeting glimpse of men with rifles coming together where another man stood. Davy called to Mitchell: "Look across to the trees! You see the feller with the red sash? Now you know who we're standin' off!"

Mitchell looked so long, Davy tapped his shoulder before the big man moved clear of the broken door and looked at Davy without saying a word.

Davy returned to the table, picked up a scrap of meat, put it in his mouth, and wiped greasy fingers on the outside of his leggings. The meat was tougher than leather. The longer he chewed it, the bigger it got. He spoke around it to the big man. "Now they got two holes to shoot through."

Mitchell placed his reloaded rifle against the wall as Davy asked why the wolf wasn't raising Cain. "He's scairt of gunfire. He'll be in the hole he dug by now. Davy, I expect it's time to leave."

Davy got rid of the bear meat before speaking. "How?"

"I got a tunnel. Come along, I'll show you." As they approached the lean-to door, Mitchell said: "Livin' like I do, with all sorts of critters willin' to get inside my fort, I figured someday they might. So I dug a tunnel from the lean-to westerly to the forest. Took six, seven months."

As the large man paused to push aside a set of wooden meat-drying racks, he said: "If they ain't found the other end."

Davy had seen other such tunnels. In places where settlers were isolated they were fairly common. Mostly they were simply deep earthen cellar-like dugouts close

166

to or beneath cabins. Tunnels of the kind Carl Mitchell had dug were not unheard of, providing there was cover at the exit end, but they required considerable back-breaking labor, more labor over long periods of time than many settlers undertook.

When Mitchell had pushed the drying racks aside, Davy saw the moth-eaten bear hide that Mitchell kicked away to reveal a dark opening. Mitchell handed his rifle to Davy. "I'll go first. It's dark down there an' the ground's wet."

The big man went feet first below the floor. When he looked up, Davy could barely make out his features. Mitchell held up a hand for the rifles. Davy passed them to him, and, as Mitchell moved deeper into the tunnel, Davy lowered himself. Mitchell was right, the ground was dank, the tunnel was darker than the inside of a boot, and smelled of rotting vegetation.

They had to crawl, but because of Mitchell's size a slighter man like Davy had plenty of head room.

They halted once for Mitchell to grope along a ledge until he found a small tin box from which he removed a candle and a flint.

The light helped but only marginally as they resumed their crawl.

CHAPTER
FOURTEEN

The Tunnel

Davy could not see around the large man and had no idea how long they had been in the tunnel until Mitchell leaned and, with the candle held close, placed a finger to his lips.

When they resumed crawling, the large man moved more slowly and occasionally paused, things that made Davy suspect that they were nearing the end of the tunnel, and he was right.

A further indication that he was correct was when he could dimly see daylight up ahead, and finally Mitchell stopped as though listening.

Davy heard nothing.

Mitchell twisted and softly said: "Horses. You hear them?"

When Davy shook his head, Mitchell resumed crawling, barely moving up to the moment he blew out the candle.

Davy finally heard a horse stamp. Around the large man he saw more light and smelled fresh air.

The last time Mitchell stopped he pushed his rifle ahead, and made a slight sound when his powder horn brushed against the gun.

Mitchell stopped moving for some time, then got belly down and inched ahead. Now Davy saw where daylight reached into the tunnel.

Mitchell stopped, crawled a yard more, stopped again and did not move. He was listening. Davy heard a horse squeal, probably a horsing mare, and gave his head a slight wag. No one in his right mind rode mares, especially if they were stalking or hiding. Every twenty-eight days mares horsed. For three days they bit other horses, kicked people, squealed, and were unpredictably obnoxious.

Mitchell inched ahead with his rifle in both hands. Davy followed. Heat reached him along with the scent of trees and underbrush.

Mitchell was lying flat out with his head and neck extended like a turtle. Davy heard him suck back a deep sweep of breath. Mitchell did not move, seemed to be scarcely breathing.

Davy's hackles rose. He did not have to be warned that there was danger outside the tunnel.

Mitchell inched back, twisted to look over one shoulder, and whispered: "Three of 'em."

"Indians?"

"Whites. One shot'll bring their friends."

Davy said: "Let me by."

Mitchell pulled away so that Davy could pass. It was a tight squeeze. Davy saw the men in buckskin, thought one looked familiar but did not dwell on this. They had rifles and knives and hatchets in their belts. The tunnel's opening had layers of autumn leaves covering most of it, which limited Davy's view, but the men standing together and gazing in the direction of the cabin were visible from the knees up.

Mitchell hissed. Davy twisted back. The large man said: "They're inside the house. I heard talk from the lean-to."

Davy faced forward. He had heard nothing. If the big man could hear in the lean-to the length of the tunnel, he had to have to hear as well as a wolf.

What Davy *did* hear was a muffled gunshot from somewhere far behind. Mitchell whispered: "Baldridge. I'll bet new money they shot Baldridge."

Davy inched ahead to watch the three renegades. Evidently they had heard the shot. They also heard something neither Davy nor his companion heard — a screech owl. Two of them muttered to the third man and started in the direction of the cabin.

Davy watched the remaining renegade, evidently told to watch the horses because, although the man strained ahead to look and listen, he did not follow the other two men.

Davy twisted and whispered to Mitchell — "One left." — and slithered past the leafy exit hole, cupped his hands, and waited for the renegade to move, which he eventually did, and Davy made the unmistakable hiss of a cotton mouth, the viper inhabitant of swampy country for which there was no antidote when he struck.

The moving renegade froze as he twisted, looking for the snake. When the man's back was to the exit hole, Davy got clear and sprang to his feet. The renegade heard leaves rustling and came around with his rifle

170

held low. He clearly thought it was the snake. He did not raise his eyes until Davy launched himself.

Without enough time to raise and cock his rifle, the renegade dropped his gun and with the upsweep of one hand drew the tomahawk from his belt. Davy hit him head-on before the renegade could raise his hatchet.

The renegade was sinewy, tough, and fought for his life with the fury of a catamount. Davy blocked the slashing hatchet, tried to roll the renegade face down, but the man arched his back in an effort to dislodge his adversary. It partially worked. Davy was pitched to one side. He used both hands to grip the renegade's hatchet wrist. When he had the arm bending earthward, he freed his right arm and struck the renegade on the jaw. The man went limp for seconds, but he was a fighter. Davy hit him again, got his own knife out, reversed it, and struck the renegade on the forehead with the weighted handle.

Mitchell came up, hatchet in hand. The renegade was bleeding and unconscious. As Davy stood up, he heard a yell. Without seeking its source he and Mitchell ran through the trees to the place several horses were tied. The animal Mitchell caught was high-headed and frightened. He had to use all his considerable strength to prevent the horse from jerking free. When he could get alongside the animal on the left side, he pulled the left rein hard enough to make the animal twist his head around. When Mitchell landed in the saddle, the horse stood dead still, little ears back.

Mitchell looked where Davy was freeing a horse. He said: "What'n hell you been doin'? They'll be after us like devils after a crippled saint. Get on the damned horse!"

When Davy was astride, Mitchell led off in a rush. They dodged trees, low limbs, and tangles of flourishing undergrowth. For a mile Davy kept pace, then he eased his mount down to a slogging trot, and again Mitchell yelled at him: "Run fer it!"

Davy did not gig the horse.

Mitchell reined up, red in the face. "What's ailin' you? They'll be after us."

Davy's answer was tersely given. "They ain't going to catch us on foot."

Mitchell's face contorted. "On foot?"

"While you was rassling with that horse, I cut the girth buckles on the other horses. First man that sticks his foot in a stirrup to rise up, the saddle will fall off atop him."

Davy offered his twist of Kentucky-cured tobacco. Mitchell was staring at him. When he eventually reached for the twist, he broke into laughter.

From this point on they favored their animals. It was still cool in the forest. Occasionally where lightning strikes had caused fires, there were clearings that the sunshine reached.

Davy held to a southerly course. He and Mitchell said very little. The big man was not entirely satisfied the renegades would not be in pursuit. Every man jack he had ever known had started life riding bareback.

When muggy warmth brought sweat, Davy's calculation put them somewhere east of the Crockett

172

clearing and maybe five or six miles from the Shoal Crossing settlement.

Finally Mitchell had time to reflect on his loss. He particularly felt sadness over the fate of his wolf. Davy put in a hopeful suggestion. "They want us. Likely they won't go back to your house an' the dog."

Mitchell did not sound encouraged when he said: "If they kill him, I swear I'll find who done it if it takes the rest of my life. Me 'n' my dog was real close."

Somewhere ahead where the country opened up and sunshine brightened the world, a gunshot sounded. Davy continued riding until the trees thinned and southward visibility was better. Then he dismounted. It was difficult to place one unexpected gunshot. He stood with his animal, waiting for the second shot. If it came, he would be able to place its location, but there was no second gunshot.

Mitchell said: "Pot hunter."

Davy led the horse until they were passing stumps. From here on they would be visible, particularly since they were moving. When Davy began edging westerly, Mitchell said he thought they should make for the settlement. Davy continued on his new course without comment; his clearing was westerly and southerly.

They heard another gunshot. Davy continued through thinned timber. Mitchell followed, alert and beginning to suspect that his companion had a reason for going in the direction of that second gunshot. He led his animal with one hand, gripped his rifle in the other hand, and constantly watched ahead and on both sides.

Davy changed course again, northward this time back into the forest. Mitchell did not say a word.

Davy finally halted. Through humid forest gloom he could see his clearing with the cabin on the east side. Across from it westerly was where the man called Mason had shot Jesse.

Mitchell stood beside Davy and jutted his jaw Indian fashion. "Yonder I expect."

Davy led off going north. He had done the same thing after Jesse had been shot — hiked northward until he was satisfied, then turned westerly, kept going in this direction until his earlier moccasin tracks veered due southward, and changed course once more.

Mitchell walked, sweated, and did not make a sound. When a third gunshot sounded, he tapped Davy's shoulder, but Davy had already seen the smoke. It came from one of the gun holes in the front wall of his cabin.

Mitchell said: "He warn't caught nappin', whoever he is."

Davy replied as he led the horse southward. "My wife or maybe my oldest boy."

"That's your place?" Mitchell asked. This time the reply was a curt nod of the head.

Where Davy finally stopped to tie the horse, Mitchell said: "It can't be them renegades we run from. They couldn't have got down here any faster'n we done."

Davy moved southward with his rifle in both hands. He did not make a sound or expose himself. He used tree cover the full distance of his stalk. Behind him the large man did the same. The fact that he was able to move without a sound and fade from sight without effort indicated that he was thoroughly accomplished at what he was doing despite being over-size in all directions.

The third gunshot came from the same fringe of forest opposite the cabin that Jesse's ambusher had used. Mitchell saw gunsmoke and grunted. They were getting close. He stopped to speak softly. "How many?"

Davy said: "He ain't alone. Scout around."

Mitchell disappeared as Davy continued forward, but only a few feet at a time from here on. When he scented dispersing gunsmoke, he stepped into a clump of underbrush, grounded his rifle, and blocked in sections of the onward gloom a square at a time.

When he saw movement, he could discern only that it was a man reloading his rifle. He was looking across the clearing in the direction of the house. Not until two more men appeared near the reloading man did Davy think this was simply one of those frequent and random attacks on an isolated homestead. One of the men who moved into view was thick, hairy, dressed like an Indian but with characteristics that meant he was white.

Davy thought he had seen this man before, but it was the second ambusher that held his attention. He knew of only one man who wore a red sash. The only way he could have come this far south so fast was if he had left the fight at Mitchell's cabin at least an hour earlier.

How the French-Canadian knew where the Crockett clearing was located was less important than the clear fact that he had known.

Baldridge had said Beaver Hat had known. Evidently what had been no mystery to Beaver Hat was no mystery to Red Sash.

Another gunshot sounded from the cabin. Davy saw the gust of burned powder smoke erupt past the gun hole.

Red Sash flinched as did the hairy man beside him. The slug must have come close. The rifleman had reloaded his piece when Davy clearly heard Red Sash say: "Fire! We go behind the cabin an' set it afire."

The kneeling man looked around from aiming. "I tol' you we'd ought to do that."

Red Sash exploded. "You don't tell Armand Breaux nothing! What do you men know? Nothing!"

The big hairy man beside Red Sash looked at the ground. It was impossible to discern through his facial hair what his reaction was to Red Sash's anger.

The rifleman got to his feet, grounded his rifle, and looked steadily at the shorter, thicker man with a brace of pistols in his sash. Davy suspected what was coming. Men like the rifleman did not like anyone different from themselves, and they would fight at the drop of a hat. The rifleman said: "You got us shot up by them Indians at the wagon fight. If you're so smart, why didn't you know them Choctaws was after the wagons, too?"

Red Sash reached for a pistol but the hairy, large man beside him knocked his hand away. He said: "Settle what we come for first. You 'n' him can settle things later. I'd like to get this done an' get clear. We're too near that settlement. By now they know what happened at the wagon fight. There'll be men swarmin' all through here."

The rifleman had one last remark to make before turning his back on Red Sash. "We started out fifteen strong. We're what's left. The others got a bellyful of you gettin' us caught and shot up."

The rifleman knelt, rested his rifle across a low limb. "What if Crockett ain't in there?"

Before Red Sash could reply, the rifleman fired, smoke rose, and Davy raised his own rifle, but, before he could find a rest and aim, a bear roared from the forest.

The buckskin-clad man beside Red Sash whirled with his rifle rising. Red Sash did not move, did not raise his rifle, did not even reach for one of the pistols in his sash. He seemed petrified.

The bear roared again. No small bear made that kind of sound. The men with Red Sash faced the forest, guns ready.

Davy settled Betsy over a limb and aimed. When he fired, Red Sash went down in a writhing heap. His companions crouched, seeking burned powder smoke. They faced in Davy's direction. Davy moved to his right, got behind a tree, and started reloading. He was ramming the ball home when the bear roared for a third time. Red Sash's companions had shot their share of bears. Both knew if the first musket ball did not penetrate the heart or brain, the bear would tear them to pieces. A bear was a very difficult animal to kill; no experienced hunter aimed for the head. A bear's skull was thick and sloping.

Davy was ready to fire again when the pair of renegades fled southward in a wild run. He only caught an occasional glimpse until they were lost amid the trees and the gloom.

Carl Mitchell called from the west. "I don't think you killed that one with the red bellyband!"

Davy almost smiled. "You'd have fooled me."

Mitchell called back. "Don't feel bad. I've fooled real bears!"

They went to the place where Red Sash was moaning and holding both bloody hands over a high leg wound. He did not look at them. He was in a sickening kind of pain.

Davy took the pistols. Mitchell took the rifle. Then they each caught hold of Red Sash and began dragging him across the clearing toward the cabin. Someone yelled from over there. Davy raised his rifle in the air to wave.

Behind them Red Sash screamed in pain. They continued to drag him until they were close to the porch, then dropped him.

Bess opened the door, rifle in hand. Behind her their children peeked like chicks behind a mother hen. Reno Knight was the last to appear. It had required time to reload Jesse's rifle that he held in both hands. He was as solemn as an owl. He pushed forward with the rifle. Without showing relief that Davy had appeared, he said: "Is he the one killed my folks?"

Davy shook his head.

Bess also moved for a closer look at the bloody man with the red sash. "Who is he?" she asked her husband.

Davy ignored the question. "Let's get him inside. Maybe you can tie off the bleeding."

Jesse appeared, pale and weak with a big girl on each side. Before he could speak, Bess turned on him: "Get back to the pallet, Mister Jones!" She faced her husband. "Why was he shooting at the house?"

CHAPTER
FIFTEEN

Settling Up

Red Sash ground his teeth as Bess worked over him. The wound was ragged so she snipped off shreds of meat, compressed the injury until she could sew it, and the oldest girl helped, white to the hairline with lips pulled flat. The bleeding would not stop.

Jesse lay nearby watching. The only comment he made was when he said: "Miz Crockett, be better if you just let him bleed out."

Davy and Carl Mitchell went outside with chunks of cooked meat in their hands. Davy said: "That big 'un. I've seen him somewhere."

Mitchell spat bone aside before replying. "Owens."

"You know that for a fact, Mister Mitchell?"

"No, sir, not for a fact, but Baldridge told me enough about him. You see, that beaded black bear paw on the back of his shirt? Baldridge told me about it. Some Indian woman put it on for him."

Davy chewed, swallowed, and gazed across the clearing. If Mitchell was right, then Owens had indeed changed sides after the wagon fight. There was nothing unusual about that. It happened every few days during the chaos of the frontier. He said: "They'd ought to be showing up directly."

Mitchell shrugged massive shoulders. "Without Red Sash I figure they'll scatter like quail." He paused in his chewing. "Them Choctaws will scatter, too. Do you know who their headman was?"

"A Creek called Charley Ben."

"The Army'll be along. They'll sweep Creek an' Choctaw country with rifles an' hang ropes." Mitchell finished his meat, wiped greasy fingers on his britches, and said: "I'll be gettin' back, Davy. I want to find my dog."

Bess came to the doorway to speak to her husband. "He's out of his head. You might want to hear."

Both men followed Bess inside and over near the fireplace where Jesse had been propped up by Reno. Nearby, Red Sash's gaze was fixed on the ceiling where children's heads crowded around the crawl hole. He said: "Masson . . . I heard he was after the wagons. I sent a scout to find him. He never come back. Masson was comin' from the north. I had to get there first. Them wagons would make all the difference."

Davy leaned. "You knew Mason?"

"Masson, not Mason. Him 'n' me come from the same country in Canada. He paid someone to know about what was in the wagons the same as I did. I don't know who he paid or how much, but Masson always had money. I had to get down here an' get hostiles to help me beat Masson to the wagons."

Davy straightened up. Bess was gently shaking her head. Mitchell leaned to ask a question. "Did you shoot my dog?"

Red Sash's breathing was coming in short bursts. "Don't know. I left to come over here."

Mitchell turned away to get some water from the dipper bucket. Davy joined him, leaving his wife kneeling beside Red Sash with Jesse Jones watching from his nearby bear-skin pallet. Red Sash continued to ramble. He occasionally spoke in a language his listeners thought was French.

Reno Knight stirred the coals, tossed on some wood, and flames flared. It was hot enough to bake bread but no one commented.

Davy went outside with Mitchell, who said he'd scout up the horses Red Sash and his companions had used. He didn't cherish the idea of the walking that would be required to get back to his cabin.

They parted with strong handclasps. Davy's final words were: "Mind, Mister Mitchell, the country's got renegades behind every tree."

Mitchell nodded as he struck out across the clearing.

The day was moving along. Davy did not return to the cabin until he'd taken Betsy on a far-around scout. What he had told Mitchell was true, with Red Sash's routed renegades, Charley Ben's wandering tomahawks, as well as other renegades passing ghost-like in all directions, Davy's country was indeed a dark and bloody ground.

When he returned to the cabin with the sun slanting away, Reno met him outside to say Red Sash had died.

Davy felt neither pity nor elation. He told the lad come sunup they'd bury him, but the following morning, as they all finished breakfast, John Wesley whistled from the porch, then ducked inside.

There were three armed men coming across the clearing from the direction of the Shoal Crossing settlement. They rode slowly and waved when Davy came outside with his rifle.

One of them was that old firebrand with unkempt hair who had got on a chair at the tavern to put forth the idea of a local militia. His name was Mike O'Brien, but he had dropped the O many years before. As he reined up in front of the house, one of his companions, who Davy did not know, solemnly untied something from his saddle and tossed it at Davy's feet. The way it landed, the beaded black bear paw was visible.

The old man said: "We never asked his name. Some fellers caught him stealin' a horse. He put up a fight. They knocked him senseless. We poured spirits into him. He said him 'n' two other fellers was fixin' to kill you. They figured you was in the house. He said you come behind them an' a feller they called Breaux was shot. They run for it." The old man shifted in the saddle, gazing at the buckskin shirt. "We hung him. You got some idea who he was, Colonel?"

Davy nodded. "His name was Owens. Him 'n' some other renegades sold lead, powder, an' guns to the Indians. There was another one run off with him."

The old man seemed less interested in Davy's explanation than he was about Davy's safety. "Did they hurt anyone, Colonel?"

"Their leader was a feller who wore a red sash. He died in my cabin. Bled out. Red Sash an' a feller named

183

Mason tried to beat each other to the Army wagons. I got between 'em, got both sides fighting one another. Do you know a Creek called Charley Ben?"

The old man shook his head.

"He was headman of some Choctaws 'n' others who met Red Sash's renegades. Him 'n' his Indians got run off."

The old man said: "That lieutenant soldier's got reinforcements from New Orleans. They're goin' to set outen to scour the country. They got a canon with 'em, an' somethin' I never seen before, a little round thing no bigger'n a ball that's full of powder. They light a fuse an' throw them things. I ain't seen one, but I've heard plenty about 'em, an', if they work, that ought to take care of renegades, red or white. He'll be comin' upcountry directly. He sent a man ahead to ask if our militia will join him as scouts. He don't know the country roundabout an' we do. Colonel, we'd be right proud if you'd join us."

Davy heard a rustling sound behind him. Bess was standing in the doorway, looking steadily and impassively at him. Frontiersmen developed powerful instincts. Davy reddened slightly as he addressed the old man. "Been gone a long spell."

From his saddle the old man also saw Bess. He considered both of them for a long moment, then raised his left hand to rein back the way he had come as he said: "It'll be maybe a week to ten days before the Army gets here. Good day to you, Colonel . . . Miz Crockett."

About the Author

Lauran Paine, who under his own name and various pseudonyms has written over a thousand books, was born in Duluth, Minnesota. His family moved to California when he was at a young age, and his apprenticeship as a Western writer came about through the years he spent in the livestock trade, rodeos, and even motion pictures, where he served as an extra because of his expert horsemanship in several films starring movie cowboy Johnny Mack Brown. In the late 1930s, Paine trapped wild horses in northern Arizona and even, for a time, worked as a professional farrier. Paine came to know the Old West through the eyes of many who had been born in the previous century, and he learned that Western life had been very different from the way it was portrayed on the screen. "I knew men who had killed other men," he later recalled. "But they were the exceptions. Prior to and during the Depression, people were just too busy eking out an existence to indulge in Saturday-night brawls." He served in the US Navy in the Second World War and began writing for Western pulp magazines following his discharge. It is interesting to note that all of his earliest novels (written under his own name and the pseudonym Mark Carrel) were published in the British market, and he soon had as strong a following in that country as in the United States. Paine's Western fiction is characterized by strong plots, authenticity, an apparently effortless ability to construct situation and character, and a preference for building his stories upon a solid foundation of historical fact. *Adobe Empire* (1956), one of his best novels, is a fictionalized account of the last twenty years in the life of trader William Bent and, in an off-trail way, has a melancholy, bittersweet texture that is not easily forgotten. In later novels like *The White Bird* (1997) and *Cache Cañon* (1998), he showed that the special magic and power of his stories and characters had only matured along with his basic themes of changing times, changing attitudes, learning from experience, respecting Nature, and the yearning for a simpler, more moderate way of life.